EX LIBRIS

VINTAGE CLASSICS

ROBERTO BOLAÑO

Roberto Bolaño was born in Santiago, Chile, in 1953. He grew up in Chile and Mexico City, where he was a founder of the Infrarealism poetry movement. Described by the *New York Times* as 'the most significant Latin American literary voice of his generation', he was the author of over twenty works, including *The Savage Detectives*, which received the Herralde Prize and the Rómulo Gallegos Prize when it appeared in 1998, and *2666*, which posthumously won the 2008 National Book Critics Circle Award for Fiction. Bolaño died in Blanes, Spain, at the age of fifty, just as his writing found global recognition.

ALSO BY ROBERTO BOLAÑO

NOVELS

The Savage Detectives

2666

Nazi Literature in the Americas

The Skating Rink

The Third Reich

Woes of the True Policeman

NOVELLAS

By Night in Chile

Distant Star

Amulet

Antwerp

Monsieur Pain

A Little Lumpen Novelita

Cowboy Graves

STORIES

Last Evenings on Earth

The Insufferable Gaucho

The Return

POETRY

The Romantic Dogs

Tres

The Unknown University

ROBERTO BOLAÑO

THE SPIRIT OF SCIENCE FICTION

TRANSLATED FROM THE SPANISH BY
Natasha Wimmer

VINTAGE CLASSICS

1 3 5 7 9 10 8 6 4 2

Vintage Classics is part of the Penguin Random House
group of companies whose addresses can be found
at global.penguinrandomhouse.com

Penguin
Random House
UK

This edition published in Vintage Classics in 2024
First published in Spain with the title *El espíritu de la ciencia-ficción* by Alfaguara in 2016
First published in the United States of America with the title
The Spirit of Science Fiction by Penguin Press in 2019

Designed by Gretchen Achilles

penguin.co.uk/vintage-classics

Printed and bound in Great Britain by Clays Ltd, Elcograf S.p.A.

The authorised representative in the EEA is Penguin Random House Ireland,
Morrison Chambers, 32 Nassau Street, Dublin D02 YH68

A CIP catalogue record for this book is available from the British Library

ISBN 9781784879549

Penguin Random House is committed to a sustainable future
for our business, our readers and our planet. This book is made
from Forest Stewardship Council® certified paper.

For Carolina López

THE
SPIRIT
OF
SCIENCE
FICTION

1

D o you mind if I interview you?"

"Go ahead, but keep it brief."

"Do you realize that you're the youngest writer ever to win this prize?"

"Is that so?"

"I've just spoken to one of the organizers. I got the sense that they were moved."

"I don't know what to tell you. . . . It's an honor. . . . I'm very happy."

"It seems everyone is happy. What are you drinking?"

"Tequila."

"Vodka here. Vodka is a strange drink, isn't it? It's not what most women would choose. Vodka neat."

"I don't know what women drink."

"Oh, no? Anyway, it doesn't matter. A woman's drink is always secret. Her true drink, I mean. Her infinite pour. But never mind. It's such a clear night, isn't it? From here we can see the farthest towns and the most distant stars."

"That's an optical illusion, miss. If you look carefully, you'll observe that the windows are oddly fogged. Go out on the terrace. I believe we're in the middle of the woods. Practically all we can see are tree branches."

"Then those are paper stars, of course. But what about the town lights?"

"Phosphorescent sand."

"You're so clever. Please, tell me about your work. Yourself and your work."

"I feel a little nervous, you know? All these people singing and dancing nonstop, I'm not . . ."

"Don't you like the party?"

"I think everyone is drunk."

"They're the winners and runners-up of all the previous prizes."

"Good God."

"They're celebrating the end of another contest. It's . . . natural."

Ghosts and ghostly days passed through Jan's mind. I think it was quick, a sigh, and then there was Jan on the floor, sweating and howling in pain. Worth mentioning, too, are the signs he was making, the frozen flurry of gestures, as if to show me that there was something on the ceiling, what? I asked as his index finger rose and fell with exasperating slowness, oh, shit, said Jan, it hurts, rats, mountain-climbing rats, you dumbfuck, and then he said, ah, ah, ah, and I grabbed him by the arms, or I pulled him up, which is when I realized that he wasn't just sweating rivers but cold rivers. I know I should have run for a doctor, but I got the sense that he didn't want to be left alone. Or maybe I was afraid to go out. (This was the night I realized that the night is really big.) Actually, from a certain perspective I think Jan didn't care whether I stayed or left. But he didn't want a doctor. So I said, don't die, you're like the prince from *The Idiot*. I'd bring you a mirror if we had a mirror, but since we don't, trust me and try to calm down, don't die on me. Then, after he had sweated a Norwegian river, he said that the roof of our room was plagued with mutant rats, can't you hear them? he whispered, my hand was on his forehead, and I said, yes, it was the first time I'd heard rats shrieking on the roof of an eighth-floor room. Ah, said Jan. Poor Posadas, he said. His body was so long and thin that I promised myself that from now on I would do a better job of keeping him fed. Then he seemed to fall asleep, his eyes half closed, his face turned to the wall. I lit a cigarette. Through our only window, the first rays of dawn began to appear. The street below was still dark and deserted, but cars went by with some regularity. Suddenly, behind me, I heard Jan's snores. I looked at him. He was asleep, naked on his bare mattress, a lock of blond hair drying slowly on his forehead. I slumped against the wall and let myself slide down until I was sitting in a corner. Through the window, I saw an airplane go by: red, green, blue, yellow lights, the kernel of a rainbow. I closed my eyes and thought about the past few days, the big sad scenes, what I could see and touch, and then I got undressed and lay down on my mattress and tried to imagine Jan's nightmares, and suddenly, before I fell asleep, I was as certain as if it was being dictated to me that Jan had felt many things that night, but not fear.

Dear Alice Sheldon:

I just want to tell you that I admire you deeply. . . . I'm a devoted reader. . . . When I had to get rid of my books (I never had a lot, but I had some), I couldn't bring myself to give away all of yours. . . . So I still have *Up the Walls of the World,* and sometimes I recite a little from memory . . . just for myself. . . . I've read your stories, too, but I gradually lost those, unfortunately. . . . Here they were published in anthologies and magazines, and some made their way to the city where I live. . . . There was a guy who loaned me rare stuff. . . . And I met a science fiction writer. . . . People say he's our only science fiction writer, but I don't believe it. . . . Remo tells me that his mother met another one, ten or fifteen years ago at least. . . . His name was González, or that's how my friend remembers it, and he worked in the records department at Valparaíso Hospital. . . . He gave money to Remo's mother and the other girls to buy his novel. . . . He published it himself with his own money. . . . González waited outside the bookstore, and Remo's mother went in and bought the book. . . . And of course the only books the store sold were the ones bought by the kids from the records department. . . . Remo remembers their names: Maite, Doña Lucía, Rabanales, Pereira. . . . But not the title of the book . . . *Martian Invasion* . . . *Flight to the Andromeda Nebula* . . . *The Secret of the Andes*. . . . I can't think what it was. . . . Maybe someday I'll find a copy. . . . After I read it, I'll send it to you as a small token of gratitude for the hours of pleasure you've given me . . .

Yours,
Jan Schrella

T hen let's talk about the winning book."

"There isn't much to say. Do you want me to tell you what it's about?"

"I'd be delighted."

"It begins in Santa Bárbara, a town near the Andes, in the south of Chile. It's a horrible place, or at least that's how I see it, nothing like these charming Mexican villages. But there's one thing that gives it class: the houses are all built of wood. I have to confess that I've never been there, but this is how I imagine it: wooden houses in every shade of brown, unpaved streets, nonexistent sidewalks—or, actually, rickety wooden ramps like in westerns, so that when it rains, mud isn't tracked inside. It's in this nightmarish, hellish Santa Bárbara that the story begins. To be precise, it begins at the Potato Academy, a kind of three-story grain shed with an iron weather vane on the roof, probably the bleakest building on Calle Galvarino and one of the many secret faculties of the Unknown University that are scattered around the world."

"Truly fascinating. Tell me more."

"On the first floor, there are just two rooms. One of them is so huge that tractors used to be kept there; the other is tiny, tucked away in a corner. In the big room, there are tables, chairs, filing cabinets, even sleeping bags and mattresses. Tacked to the walls are posters and drawings of different kinds of tubers. The small room is empty. It's a room with a floor, a ceiling, wooden walls—not old wood from when the grain shed was built but new wood, neatly cut and polished, nearly jet-black. I'm not boring you, am I?"

"No, go on, go on. This is a nice break for me. You wouldn't believe all the interviews I had in Mexico City this morning. They work us like slaves at the paper."

"All right. On the second floor, reached by stairs without a handrail, there are two more rooms, each of the same size. In one of them, there are a few mismatched chairs, a desk, a blackboard, and other items that give the room the vague feel of a classroom. In the other room, there's nothing but rusty old farm equipment. Finally, on the third floor, which is reached from the tool room, we find a ham radio set and a profusion of maps scattered on the floor, a small FM transmitter, some semiprofessional recording equipment, a set of Japanese amplifiers, et cetera. I say et cetera because anything that I haven't mentioned either isn't important or else will be described later in full detail."

"My dear friend, the suspense is killing me."

"Spare me the ironic commentary. As I was saying, the third floor, which is actually a huge single attic room, is scattered with all of these modern or quasi-modern communication devices. The ham radio set is the only surviving piece of a collection of equipment that the academy once used for teaching purposes but that had to be sold due to general neglect by the UU and because the caretaker needed to eat. The room is a complete mess; it looks as if no one has bothered to sweep or mop for months. There are a couple of windows with wooden shutters, too few for the size of the room. From the eastward-facing one, you see the mountains. From the other, the view is of an endless forest and the beginning or the end of a path."

"An idyllic landscape."

"Idyllic or terrifying, depending how you look at it."

"Hmm . . ."

"The academy is surrounded by a yard. In the old days, it was full of carts and trucks. Now the only vehicle in the yard is a BMX bike belonging to the caretaker, a man in his sixties; he's a health nut, hence the bicycle. Around the yard is a wooden-and-wire fence. There are only two entrances. The main gate is big and heavy, and on the front of it is a yellowish metal sign stamped with black letters reading POTATO ACADEMY—ALIMENTARY RESEARCH 3, and beneath, in tiny print, the street name and number: 800 GALVARINO. The other door is in what a normal visitor would call the backyard. This door is small, and instead of opening onto the street it leads into a vacant lot and beyond to the woods and the path."

"The same path you can see from the attic?"

"Yes, the tail end of it."

"It must be nice to live in an attic, even a tiny one."

"I lived in a rooftop room for centuries. I don't recommend it."

"I didn't say a rooftop room, I said an attic."

"Same thing. The view is the same. A view of the gallows, but with depth. With sunrises and sunsets."

It was the ideal scene on which to pin images or desires, I thought—a young man, five foot eight, in jeans and a blue T-shirt, standing in the sun on the curb of the longest street in the Americas.

This meant that we were in Mexico at last and that the sun shining down on me between buildings was the sun of the Mexico City I'd dreamed of for so long. I lit a cigarette and searched for our window. The building where we lived was greenish gray, like the uniform of the Wehrmacht, Jan had said three days ago, when we found the room. There were flowers on the apartment balconies. Higher up—smaller than some flowerpots—were the windows of the rooftop rooms. I was tempted to call Jan to come to the window and see our future. And then what? Skip out of there, say, Jan, I'm off, I'll pick up avocados for lunch (and milk, though Jan hated milk), and good news, super queer, perfect poise, eternal faggot in the antechambers of greatness, I'll be star reporter of the poetry section, every telephone at my disposal.

Then my heart began to hammer strangely. I thought, I'm a statue frozen between the road and the sidewalk. I didn't scream. I walked on. Seconds later, when I had yet to emerge from the shadow of our building or the weave of shadows that covered this stretch, my reflection appeared in the windows of Sanborns, strange mental duplication—a young man with long hair in a ripped blue T-shirt who bowed, genuflecting strangely before the jewels and the crimes (but what jewels and what crimes I forgot immediately) with rolls and avocados in my arms, and a liter of Lala milk, and the eyes, not my eyes but eyes lost in the black hole of the window, narrowed as if they had suddenly seen the desert.

I turned around slowly. I knew it. Jan was watching me from the window. I waved my arms in the air. Jan shouted something unintelligible and leaned farther out. I jumped. Jan responded by moving his head back to front and then in circles, faster and faster. I was afraid that he would throw himself out the window. I started to laugh. The passersby stared at me, and then they looked up and saw Jan, who was lifting his leg, pretending to kick a cloud. He's my friend, I said. We just moved here a few days ago. He's wishing me luck. I'm on my way out to look for work. Oh, well, that's nice, what a good friend, someone said, and walked on, smiling.

I believed that nothing bad would ever happen to us in that welcoming city. How near and how far from what fate had in store for me! How sad and transparent that first Mexican smile appears now in memory!

I dreamed about a Russian guy. . . . What do you think of that?"

"I don't know. . . . I dreamed about a blond girl. . . . It was getting dark. . . . Like on the outskirts of Los Ángeles, but pretty soon it wasn't Los Ángeles anymore. It was Mexico City, and the girl was walking in clear plastic tunnels. . . . She had sad eyes. . . . But that was yesterday, on the bus."

"In my dream, the Russian was happy. Somehow I could tell that he was going to go up in a spaceship."

"Then it was Yuri Gagarin."

"More tequila?"

"*Ándele*, pal, *simonel*."

"At first I thought it was Yuri Gagarin, too, but you won't believe what happened next. . . . In the dream, it made my hair stand on end."

"You were sleeping soundly, though. I was writing until late, and you looked fine."

"Well, then the Russian got into his space suit and turned

his back on me. He left. I wanted to go after him, but I don't know what was wrong with me; I couldn't walk. Then the Russian turned and waved good-bye. . . . And you know what he looked like, what he was?"

"No . . ."

"A dolphin . . . there was a dolphin inside the suit. . . . My hair bristled, and I wanted to cry . . ."

"But you weren't even snoring."

"It was terrible. . . . It doesn't seem like it now, but in the dream it was awful, like a knot in my throat. It wasn't death, you know? It was more like erasure."

"The dolphin of Leningrad."

"I think it was an omen. . . . You didn't sleep?"

"No, I wrote all night."

"Are you cold?"

"Extremely. Fuck, I thought it would never be cold here."

"The sun is coming up."

Our heads barely fit in the window frame. Jan said he'd thought about Boris. He said it in an offhand way.

The sunrise said: I'm out of this world. Get used to it. Once every three days, you'll be seeing me.

"Jesus, what a sunrise," said Jan, his eyes wide and his hands in fists.

I started to do work for the arts supplement of the newspaper *La Nación*. The supplement's editor, Rodríguez, an old Andalusian poet who had been a friend of Miguel Hernández, let me write something for each issue. Once a week, in other words. With what I made on four pieces a month, we could get by for eight or nine days. The other twenty-one days, we lived off the articles I wrote for a magazine of pseudohistory run by an Argentinean just as old as Rodríguez, though he had the smoothest, most flawless skin I'd ever seen. People called him "the Doll," for obvious reasons. The rest was put up by my parents or Jan's parents. It worked out more or less like this: 30 percent of the money came from *La Nación,* another 30 percent from our parents, and 40 percent from *History and Society,* which was the name of the Doll's misbegotten creation. I could turn out the four assignments for *La Nación* in a couple of days; they were reviews of poetry books, a few novels, and the occasional essay collection. Rodríguez gave me the books on Saturday mornings, which was when everyone, or almost everyone, who wrote for the supplement gathered in the tiny cubicle that served as the old man's office, handing in assignments, picking up checks, and proposing ideas that must have been really bad, or if not, maybe Rodríguez had rejected them, because the supplement was always the worst rag. The real reason people came on Saturdays was to talk to their friends and bad-mouth their enemies. They were all poets, they all drank, they were all older than me. It wasn't much fun, but I never missed a Saturday. When Rodríguez wrapped things up, we went to the cafés and talked until, one by one, the poets went back to their jobs and I was left alone at the table, legs crossed, watching the view through the window: the boys and girls of Mexico City, ecstatic policemen, and a sun that seemed to keep watch over the planet from the rooftops. With the Doll, things were different. First of all, pride—it makes me blush now—led me to refuse to publish any pieces under my own name. When I told the Doll this, he blinked, hurt, but agreed. What do you want to call yourself, kid? He grunted. Without hesitation, I said, Antonio Pérez. I see, said the Doll. You have literary ambitions. No, I swear I don't, I said, lying. Whether you do or not, I'm going to demand quality work from you, he said. And then, more sadly, to think of all the pretty stories you can write on these topics. My first piece was on Dillinger. The second was on the Naples Camorra. (Antonio Pérez went so far as to quote entire paragraphs from a Conrad story!) Then came the St. Valentine's Day Massacre, the life of a poisoner from Walla

Walla, the Lindbergh kidnapping, et cetera. The offices of *History and Society* were in an old building in Colonia Lindavista, and the entire time I was bringing in work, I never saw anyone but the Doll. Our meetings were short: I turned in the pieces, and he gave me new assignments and loaned me reference material, photocopies of magazines that he had published in his native Buenos Aires and photocopies of sister magazines from Spain and Venezuela that I used as sources but also sometimes shamelessly plagiarized. Occasionally the Doll asked about Jan's parents—they were old friends—and then he sighed. How is the Schrellas' son? Fine. What's he doing? Nothing, he's in school. Ah. And that was all. Jan, it goes without saying, wasn't in school, though we fed the lie to his parents to keep them quiet. Actually, Jan never left the room. He spent all day there doing God knows what. He did go out to the toilet or the shower that we shared with the other roof tenants, and sometimes he went down to take a walk along Insurgentes, two blocks at most, moving slowly and seeming to sniff around for something, and very soon he was back. Meanwhile I was lonely; I needed to meet other people. The solution came from a poet at *La Nación* who worked on the sports section. He said: go to the poetry workshop at the Faculty of Literature. He said: you'll find young people there, people your own age, not shitty drunks and has-beens who just want to be on a payroll somewhere. I smiled. Now the old bastard is going to cry, I thought. He said: poetesses, there are poetesses there, kid, get in on the action. Ah.

Dear James Hauer:

I read in a Mexican magazine that you're planning
to form a committee of American science fiction writers
in support of Third World countries, especially Latin
America. It's not a bad idea, maybe a little vague, though
the magazine's reporting may be more to blame for that
than your proposal. Just so you know, I'm a Latin
American science fiction writer. I'm seventeen, and I
have yet to see anything I've written in print. I did show
a few stories to a teacher of mine back home, a decent
man, madly in love with Scott Fitzgerald (and, in a calmer
way, the Republic of Letters) as only a reader from one of
our Latin American countries can be. Think of a
pharmacist from the Deep South or someone stuck in a
small town in Arizona, a fanatic admirer of Vachel
Lindsay, and you'll get the idea. Or not and just keep
reading. Anyway, as I was saying, I delivered my
gibberish into the hands of this person, and I waited.

When he had read my story, the good man said: dear Jan,
I hope you haven't been smoking. He was referring
erroneously to marijuana, which as far as I know doesn't
cause hallucinations, but he meant that he hoped I wasn't
fucking myself up on acid or something. (I have to warn
you that in high school I had a reputation as a bright
student, though prone to "absentmindedness" and
"distraction.") Sir, I said, it's a science fiction story. The
man thought for a few seconds. But, Jan, he replied, those
things are so remote. His index finger drifted upward in
a northwesterly direction and then almost straight down
south, poor tremor-afflicted soul, or poor mind of mine,
which even back then could be rattled and unfocused by
Reality. Most respected sir, I argued, if you believe that
we can't write about interplanetary travel, for example,
you leave us at the mercy of the dreams—and
amusements—of others, *in saecula saeculorum;* notice,
too, that my characters are Russian, which isn't a random
choice at all. Our dream, spluttered my never-too-
esteemed teacher, should be 1928 France. Since I didn't
quite know what had happened in Paris that year, I took
this to be the end of our conversation. The next day, when
we met again at school, I said: teacher, someday you're
going to get fucked up the ass by 1939 France, lock, stock,
and barrel. If I'd been able to read the future, such an
insult surely would never have passed my lips. My
oft-remembered teacher died just a few months later
when he went for a walk by the light of the moon after

curfew. The stories, meanwhile, were lost. So do you think that we have any hope of writing good science fiction? Will your committee, God bless it, award grants—Hugo grants, Nebula grants—to the Third World natives who do the best job describing robots? Or maybe the group that you head proposes to testify on our behalf—in solidarity, of course—on the political stage? I await your immediate response.

Affectionately,
Jan Schrella

The workshop was led by Jeremías Moreno, prizewinning poet, and it was held in a small room on the third floor of the Faculty of Literature. On one wall, someone had written ALCIRA SOUST SCAFFO WAS HERE in red spray paint, ten inches from the floor, clear but unobtrusive, impossible to see if the visitor didn't look down. Though at first glance the graffiti seemed completely innocent, after a few minutes of repeated reading it began to feel like a shout, an agonizing display. Judging by the paint, it wasn't recent, and I wondered who could have written it, what good fairy had rescued it from the vigilantes of good manners, who this Alcira was who had set up camp a few inches from the floor.

To make things even more confusing, Jeremías asked me in a whisper what I wanted. I explained, maybe too eagerly, that Colin, the baseball expert at *La Nación*, had recommended his workshop to me. I used the words "advice" and "suggestion"; I was about to precede them with the adjectives "brilliant" and "happy," but I was halted by his expression of complete bafflement. It had been only a few seconds, and everyone hated me already.

"Never heard of the man."

"Short, dark . . . big nose," I stammered.

"No clue."

We were silent for a moment. I think it was the graffiti, the magnetic attraction of those red letters—which for some reason I immediately associated with poverty and kindness—that kept me from fleeing. I can't remember when exactly Jeremías Moreno asked me to sit down or when he made the obligatory remarks about the country I was from. The members of the workshop had arranged their chairs in a circle, broken only by the door. There were no girls among the apprentice poets, I noted with a surge of discouragement, heightened, if possible, upon scanning their faces and discovering that not a single one of them looked like someone I'd want to get to know.

Who's reading first? A skinny kid passed out three copies of a poem. I didn't get one, but by craning my neck I could read the title on my neighbor's copy. "The Willow," said the kid. Heh-heh, it's metaphysical, kind of. Go on, then. Threatened by a creeping mental fog, I counted twenty lines the way an insomniac counts sheep. Or maybe thirty. Or maybe fifteen kicks planted on the writer's backside, followed by a silence, and some "hmm"s, some coughs, some faint smiles, some "uh-huh"s. I get the sense, said a fat kid, that you're trying to con us. The rhythm, I think. No, it's the gerunds—there should never be two in a row. And why all the "and"s?

To make it more powerful. Make the willow more powerful. Fucking college kids, I thought. I learned everything I know from Mariano Pérez, said the author, trapped. (Mariano Pérez, as I later learned, was Jeremías's buddy and the co-ordinator of the *other* workshop, the *official* Faculty of Literature workshop.) Is that so? said Jeremías resentfully. Well, I still think it sounds bad, said the fat kid. I know for a fact that you've done better work. Actually, to me it sounds like Frost, broke in a kid with glasses. Jeremías almost erupted. The only Frost you've read is in anthologies, you bonehead. Let me see, read that line again, the one about the willow weeping. T. S. Eliot? Bonifaz Nuño? Mariano? Let's not implicate Mariano in this crime, please. Interesting the way the lines are arranged, said the kid with glasses. Jeremías grabbed a copy from the poet next to him. If you turn it upside down and look hard at it, it could be a willow. Spatial arrangement, I suppose—Jean-Clarence Lambert? I swear it's a coincidence. Maybe you're just a bad reader, said Jeremías, conciliatory and weary of the discussion. Who wants to read it again? You do it, Jeremías, you're the best reader. All right, then. Ahem, let's give it a try. Does the willow remember its horizon? Why, yes—crocodile smile—there's a hint of Mariano here, no doubt about it. That's because Mariano is my model. I can see that. Look, cut the first twenty lines and keep the ending, it's really powerful. Who wants to read next?

The kids shuffled through their papers, reluctant. Jeremías consulted his watch with the professional flourish of a psychoanalyst. I heard shouts from the hall, voices, kids calling good-bye, doors slamming, until another poet, one who had so far opened his mouth only to exhale cigarette smoke, passed out three copies, like the first kid.

When the reading was over, everyone nodded in the same blissful state. Man, you're really improving, Márquez, said Jeremías. But try not to bring up *love* so much—it makes you sound like Horace. I think our friend Márquez is in love. Ha-ha-ha. Nods of agreement were followed by gripes about Márquez's luck. Nice poem, yes sir. In gratitude, the object of this praise passed around a pack of Camels previously kept under lock and key in the pocket of his sweatshirt. Carefully, I lit a cigarette, and I smiled because everyone was smiling. This kind of workshop, I thought, was like a tiny dance club for shy, boring people, though as I would soon have occasion to learn, I was gravely mistaken. Didn't you bring in anything else, Márquez? No, that's all I typed up. Did you really like it? It's a good poem: unpretentious, epigrammatic, forceful, declared Jeremías. Márquez's face changed colors, a strange soup of mingled pride and vulnerability.

What did I think about then? I thought about food, about Jan on the roof, about the Mexican buses that ply their routes through the night, about Boris, about me sitting sadly in this creepy little room. But I didn't budge, and it was a good thing I didn't. Because suddenly the door opened and a stranger in grease-stained jeans and black leather boots joined the group, saying hello and standing there, his back to me, as the poets shifted uneasily in their chairs and Jeremías said good evening, José, outwardly deferential, though wishing

26

terrible misfortune on him with eyes and eyebrows. His very black hair fell past his shoulders, and he had a book crammed in the back pocket of his pants like the reactor on a ship. I knew he was a kamikaze. But I also knew that he could be many other things, among them a voyager through the writing workshops springing up around the city, though in them he would clearly be out of place. He was oblivious of the mocking looks that the poets exchanged, possibly amused when everyone hurried to make room for him (between a pensive literature student and me), unruffled when asked whether something had happened to him, whether he'd brought poems, whether he'd been out of town, whether he'd read the latest book by.

He smiled and said no, he hadn't been away, hadn't been in an accident, hadn't brought in anything written—much less in triplicate—but not to worry, he had a good memory.

"I'm going to recite something for you. It's a poem I'm calling 'Eros and Thanatos.'"

Then he lay back in his chair, fixed his eyes on the ceiling, and began to speak.

The caretaker of the academy is an energetic man. He sleeps on the second floor of the academy, and he takes his lunch at a house in town. Whenever he leaves the grain shed, it's on the BMX. At night, he makes something to eat on the camp stove while broadcasting folk music over the radio. When he's done eating, he makes a cup of tea and smokes a cigarette. Only then does he sit down in front of the microphone. His live broadcast isn't very interesting. Lectures on how to double or triple potato crops, how to cook potatoes one hundred ways, how to make potato soup or potato jam, how to store potatoes for five years or even ten, et cetera. His voice is calm, relaxed: he speaks coolly but in the confidence-inspiring tone of a man of reason. I don't know how many people listen to him. It can't be more than a few. There are no listener surveys in the region. But anyone who listens carefully will realize, sooner or later, that his voice isn't just detached or lazy but unmistakably icy. When the program is over, he smokes another cigarette and records his observations of the day in a kind of log. Then he starts the tape recorder. The tape spins silently, and the man falls asleep in his chair or pretends to be asleep."

"Are the tapes playing or recording?"

"I don't know. The man, I should say, pretends to sleep, but he's actually listening to sounds. The grain shed creaks endlessly all night long, each gust of wind is answered by a particular faint moan of timbers, and the man's ear is tuned to the wind and the sounds of the grain shed. Until he gets bored. Sometimes he dreams about Boris."

"So he doesn't listen all night long?"

"No. He gets bored and goes to sleep. The tape rolls on, of course. When the caretaker wakes up around eight, he turns it off and rewinds. Really, there's nothing fun about life at the Academy. The scenery is nice and the air is healthy, but it's not a fun life, no matter how the caretaker tries to fill his hours with petty pursuits. Among these occupations, let's single out three: the nightly didactic potato lectures, the silent tape recorder, and the ham radio set. This last activity is even more fruitless than the rest, if possible. Basically, the caretaker searches the airwaves for a message that never comes. But, oh, his patience is infinite, and every day, once every eight hours, he issues his call: 'HWK, do you receive me? HWK, do you receive me? Academy here, HWK, academy here, academy here . . .'"

"And no one answers."

"No. The man searches, but no one answers. Very occasionally, he picks up distant voices, maybe other ham radio

29

operators, stray words, but mostly all he hears is the buzz of static. Sounds like fun, doesn't it?"

"Well . . ."

"It's a riot. The poor caretaker has a heavy Chilean accent. Imagine him talking to himself in his high voice: 'HWK, do you receive me? HWK, do you receive me?' Ha-ha-ha . . . Straight-faced . . ."

Dear Forrest J Ackerman:

   I'd been asleep for only half an hour when Thea
von Harbou appeared. I opened my eyes and said I'm
freezing, I never thought I'd be cold in this part of the
world. (Somewhere there was a blanket, but it wasn't
within arm's reach.) She was standing by the door, next
to a poster that Remo brought home a little while ago. I
closed my eyes and said to her: tell me where I am, really.
Through the window came narrow beams of light, the
reflection of distant buildings or maybe the Tecate sign
turning on and off all night. Am I alone? I asked, and she
smiled without moving from the door, her huge, deep eyes
fixed on the corner where I was trying to stop shivering.
This went on for a while, I don't know how long. At some
point, I remembered something, and I started to cry.
Then I looked her in the face, and I said you see, I'm
crying it's so cold. Where the hell is my blanket? I was
so very sad, and I was whimpering. I don't know what I

wanted her to do: open the door and go back to her cloud
or come and wipe away my tears. I smiled at her. Her
cheekbones gleamed, and she looked like a pillar of salt.
Thea von Harbou, I said, tell me where I am, really. Has
the war begun yet? Are we all cracked? She didn't answer,
but it didn't last long. I looked at Remo's alarm clock: it
was three in the morning. (My eye was reflected in the
face of the clock.) At three-ten, I woke up and made
myself a cup of tea. Now it's four, and I'm waiting for
the sun to rise, writing you this letter. I've never read
anything by you, Mr. Ackerman, except that horrible
preface in which some evil editor calls you Mr. Science
Fiction. Maybe you're dead, too, and at Ace Books, where
I'm writing to you, no one even remembers you. But since
I'm guessing you still love Thea von Harbou, I'm writing
you these lines. What was she like in my dream? She was
blond. She had big eyes, and she was wearing a WWI
lamé dress. Her skin was luminous, I don't know, it hurt
me. In the dream, I imagined it was skin beyond repair.
Honestly, it was hard to stop looking at her.

Warmly,

Jan Schrella

efore we move on to more important matters, I should talk to you about Dr. Huachofeo. He isn't an important figure, but he is indispensable. And ornamental. He's like the coat of paint on a crossbeam. I don't know if you follow me. A ray of light, a pocket-size Joselito for our pains . . ."

"Is that a tear in your eye? Young as you are, you remember Joselito, too?"

"Yes, but never mind that. Instead you should ask me what was in the academy file cabinets."

"Go on, then, tell me."

"The cabinets were full of the potato lectures that the caretaker broadcast over the radio or delivered personally when there were still students who came to the grain shed. None of the papers had dates. There were no names. Just the courses taught, filed by trimester, several three-year cycles' worth of them. To judge by the papers, the old caretaker was responsible for the education of several classes of experts on the potato as staple."

"I hate potatoes. They're fattening."

"Ask me what books were in the grain shed."

"Let's hear it."

"If we exclude the manuals and textbooks, all relating to the world of the potato, we are left with just one: *The Paradoxical History of Latin America,* by Pedro Huachofeo, B.A. in economics and M.D. in veterinary science, both degrees obtained at the University of Los Ángeles in the province of Bío-Bío. A five-hundred-page tome, lavishly illustrated by the author himself and full of stories, half of which don't take place in Latin America."

"The name sounds familiar."

"Huachofeo, I should say, was the pseudonym of a scion of one of the richest landowning families, which disinherited him, of course. He was killed in a raid at a brothel down south."

"Ah, always the violence. And the machismo. Why do our intellectuals have to be such creeps when it comes to sex?"

"You're wrong. Huachofeo was there to receive a message. His contact didn't show up, and the poor guy sat for a while talking to a pimp and sipping some tasty house red. Pure bad luck."

"Uh-huh. The caretaker was a friend of Huachofeo's, I suppose."

"No—an admirer. Or a student of his work, if you prefer. The caretaker believed that the meanderings and ponderings of *The Paradoxical History of Latin America* were really signals in code. But let's leave Dr. Huachofeo in his grave. As you'll see, there are many coded messages. I'm telling you all this because the soul of the dead author, present in this book—the only nonacademic book read by the caretaker—roamed the academy, along with other ghosts. It was one of the guardian spirits of the academy. And that's all. That's the Potato Academy. Where Boris studied."

"I'm going to get myself another vodka."

"Bring me a tequila or whatever while you're up."

"Wonderful. Now you look happier."

The name of the author of "Eros and Thanatos" was José Arco. Before the night was over, we were friends. The kids from the workshop asked me out for coffee, and José Arco came, too. I rode in one of the poets' cars; he rode behind us—but also beside and sometimes ahead of us—on a black Honda. I was surprised: in those days, more and more motorcycles were turning up in poems, but there weren't many poets on real motorcycles on real streets; also, as I could see from the car window, he rode in a particular way. Hardly the inscrutable biker, he made his presence known with hand signals and waves and cries, attuned not just to the nocturnal landscape but also, I could have sworn, to the ghosts—half vision and half apparition—that appear behind trees and on cracked sidewalks in the old neighborhoods of Mexico City. Later, when everyone had gone and he and I were still eating and drinking, he confessed that his motorcycle had broken down and that he was actually happy about it, since he was a walker by nature. I asked no questions until we left the bar. The motorcycle, in fact, wouldn't start, and we decided to leave it parked in front of the house we liked best. Actually, it was he who asked me if I liked the looks of some houses that he pointed out not entirely at random as we pushed the motorcycle along, while at the same time begging me to be honest and not weasel out and choose any old house. The fourth received my nod of approval. This is where Teresa lives, he said with a smile. The street, José Arco, the motorcycle, me—together we formed a strange unit. Our shadows, too dark, stretched to a wizened and nearly leafless oak; from the distance came snatches of a song. I whispered, happy: Who is Teresa?

"A friend."

"Let's go see her and tell her we've left the motorcycle here."

"No," said José Arco, "she'll realize in the morning, when she wakes up."

"Call her on the phone, then."

"No, it's too late, let's go."

It didn't take a genius to realize that he was in love and that the motorcycle parked in front of the house was some kind of offering. I didn't say anything, and we walked away. Deep down I was incredibly happy to have chosen the house of the only person he knew in the neighborhood. From where we were in Colonia Coyoacán, it was blocks and blocks to my rooftop room, and there would be plenty of time to talk. At first José Arco wasn't very communicative, or rather he was semicommunicative: he muttered incomprehensible

37

things, assumed that you knew what he was talking about, had trouble explaining his stories, talked as if desperation and happiness were the same thing, a single territory, the site of his Language Academy and his homeland. And so, little by little, on this walk and later ones, he gave me a summary of his life. We were the same age, twenty-one. He had studied sociology and philosophy and hadn't gotten a degree in either. An illness, which he didn't like to talk about, had caused him to drop out of school. He had spent four months in the hospital. One morning a doctor told him that he should have been dead two weeks ago. José Arco said that then he leaned on one elbow and struck the doctor with a right cross, the first time he'd punched anybody. When he went back to school, his friends, who by now were in their second year, explained in some disappointment that all this time they'd thought he was in the mountains with the guerrilla troops of the Party of the Poor. He stuck it out for two days, and then he decided he'd had enough. At the time, he was living in a house in Satélite with his mother and his little brother, Gustavito, a six-foot-tall giant of a kid. I'll have more to say about his mother later. There's not much to tell about Gustavito: I think he wanted to study law, and maybe he's a lawyer by now, though José tried more than once to convince him that he was the great hope of Mexican heavyweights, the avenger of Pulgarcito Ramos, just what Satélite needed to come out swinging and shut down the competition from Tepito and La Bondojito. His brother, benevolent and patient as only a two-hundred-pound adolescent can be, laughed and let him talk. I think José Arco loved his family much more than he let on. (His father is the invisible man in this story.) Then he enrolled in the philosophy department and began to go to class again almost every day. Like so many others, he hung out at film clubs and went to parties thrown by the heroes of the day. He found work as a proof-reader at a publishing house and stopped going to class; this time he and the university parted ways permanently. He left home at nineteen, almost twenty, and spent his time rolling around Mexico City dreaming up weird projects, planning swift and meticulous scenes that left him suddenly exhausted, racked, straddling the motorcycle pulled to a halt wherever he happened to be, gripping the handlebars so as not to fall off. Thanks to him, I got to know the dens of San Juan de Letrán, the neighborhoods around Garibaldi where we sold Virgin of Guadalupe lamps on the installment plan, the chop shops of Peralvillo, the dusty rooms of Romero Rubio, the shady photography studios of Avenida Misterios, the hole-in-the-wall eateries behind Tepeyac that we reached by motor-cycle as the sun was beginning to rise over the neighborhood, which looked just as cheerful and unsavory to us as we did to the women who served us pozole. Back then he was king of the frogs and I was ambassador of the rats, and our friend-ship and our schemes were in full swing. Many were the nights we spent in the rooftop room with Jan, whom he loved from the start. Sometimes he came by late, at three or four in the morning, waking us up with a long cry, like a wolf, and then Jan leaped up from his mattress, went over to the window, and said: it's José Arco. Other times we were awake, reading or writing, and he came up with a bottle of tequila and three ham sandwiches, with Posada and Remedios Varo postcards for Jan's correspondence, with poetry books and little magazines, with reports on the cloud, the eye that was advancing on Mexico City. Don't scare me, I said. Jan laughed. He loved José Arco's visits. José Arco sat down on the floor and asked me what article I was perpetrating for the Doll, and then he talked science fiction with Jan. The sandwiches, wrapped in brown paper, were enormous and full of everything: beans, tomato, lettuce, sour cream, avocado, chile pepper, and two slices of ham. The little bottle of tequila was finished before the sandwiches, and we would end the evening drinking tea, playing some radio show with the volume turned way down, reading poetry, Jan translating poems by Daniel Biga or Marc Cholodenko, whom José Arco would meet many years later, but that's another story; at six thirty or seven, he said good-bye, took the stairs one by one, got on his Honda, and disappeared down Insurgentes. We went back to our mattresses and fell asleep, and sometimes I dreamed that José Arco was gliding on his black motorcycle along a frozen avenue, without a glance at the icicles that hung from the windows, shivering with cold, until suddenly, from a sky that was also white and frozen, came a blazing red lightning bolt, and houses and streets split apart, and my friend disappeared in a kind of hurricane of mud. When I woke up, it was usually with a sharp headache.

Yesterday I dreamed about Thea von Harbou. . . . It woke me right up. . . . But then, thinking about it, I realized that I dreamed about her because of a novel I read recently. . . . It's not that it was such a strange book, but I got the idea that the author was hiding something. . . . And after the dream, I figured it out . . ."

"What novel?"

"*Silhouette,* by Gene Wolfe."

". . ."

"Want me to tell you what it's about?"

"All right, while I'm making breakfast."

"I had some tea before, when you were asleep."

"I've got a headache. Are you going to want another cup of tea?"

"Yes."

"Go on. I'm listening, even if my back is turned."

"It's the story of a spaceship that for a long time has been looking for a planet habitable by the human race. At last they find one, but it's been many years since they set off on the voyage, and the crew has changed; they've all gotten older, but you have to realize that they were very young when they set off. . . . What's changed are their beliefs: sects, secret societies, covens have sprung up. . . . The ship has also fallen into disrepair—there are computers that don't work, blown-out lights that no one bothers to fix, wrecked sleeping compartments. . . . Then, when they find the new planet, the mission is completed and they're supposed to return to Earth with the news, but no one wants to go back. . . . The voyage will consume the rest of their youth, and they'll return to an unknown world, because meanwhile several centuries have gone by on Earth, since they've been traveling at close to light speed. . . . It's just a starving, overpopulated planet. . . . And there are even those who believe that there is no life left on Earth. . . . Among them is Johann, the protagonist. . . . Johann is a quiet man, one of the few who love the ship. . . . He's of average height. . . . There's a hierarchy of height; the woman who's captain of the ship, for example, is the tallest, and the privates are the shortest. . . . Johann is a lieutenant; he goes about his duties without making too many friends. Like nearly everyone, he's set in his ways; he's bored . . . until they reach the strange planet. . . . Then Johann discovers that his shadow has grown darker. . . . Black as outer space and dense . . . As you probably guessed, it's not his shadow but a separate being that's taken cover there, mimicking the movements of his shadow. . . . Where has it come from? The planet? Space? We'll never know, and it doesn't really matter. . . . The Shadow is powerful, as we'll see, but as silent as Johann. . . . Meanwhile the sects are preparing to mutiny. . . . A group tries to convince Johann to join them; they tell him that he's one of the chosen, that their common fate is to create something new on this planet. . . . Some seem pretty loony, others dangerous. . . . Johann commits to nothing. . . . Then the Shadow transports him to the planet. . . . It's a vast jungle, a vast desert, a vast beach. . . . Johann, dressed only in shorts and sandals, almost like a Tyrolean, walks through the undergrowth. . . . He moves his right leg when he feels the Shadow push against his right leg, then the left, slowly, waiting. . . . The darkness is total. . . . But the Shadow looks after him as if he's a child. . . . When he returns, rebellion breaks out. . . . It's total chaos. . . . Johann, as a precaution, takes off his officer's stripes. . . . Suddenly he runs into Helmuth, the captain's favorite and one of the heads of the rebellion, who tries to kill him, but the Shadow overpowers him, choking him to death. . . . Johann realizes what's happening and makes his way to the bridge; the captain and some of the other officers are there, and on the screens of the central computer they see Helmuth and the mutineers readying a laser cannon. . . . Johann convinces them that all is lost, that they must flee to the planet. . . . But at the last minute, he stays behind. . . . He returns to the bridge, disconnects the fake video feed that the computer operators have manipulated, and sends an ultimatum to the rebels. . . . Whoever lays down arms this very instant will be pardoned; the rest will die. . . . Johann is well

acquainted with the tools of falsehood and propaganda. . . .
Then, too, he has the police and the marines on his side,
who've spent the voyage in hibernation, and he knows that
no one can snatch victory from him. . . . He finishes his com-
muniqué with the announcement that he is the new
captain. . . . Then he plots another route and abandons the
planet. . . . And that's all. . . . But then I dreamed about Thea
von Harbou, and I realized that it was a Millennial Reich
ship. . . . They were all Germans . . . all trapped in entropy. . . .
Though there are a few weird things, strange things. . . .
Under the effects of some drug, one of the girls—the one
who sleeps most often with Johann—remembers something
painful, and, weeping, she says that her name is Joan. . . . The
girl's real name is Grit, and Johann thinks that maybe her
mother called her Joan when she was a baby. . . . Old-fangled
and unfashionable names, banned by the psychologists,
too . . ."

"Maybe the girl was trying to say that her name was
Johann."

"Possibly. The truth is, Johann is a serious fucking
opportunist."

"So why doesn't he stay on the planet?"

"I don't know. Leaving the planet, and not going back to
Earth, is like choosing death, isn't it? Or maybe the Shadow
convinced him that he shouldn't colonize the planet. Either
way, the captain and a bunch of people are stuck there. Listen, read the novel, it's really good. . . . And now I think the

swastika came from the dream, not Gene Wolfe. . . . Though who knows . . . ?"

"So you dreamed about Thea von Harbou . . ."

"Yes, it was a blond girl."

"But have you ever seen a picture of her?"

"No."

"How did you know it was Thea von Harbou?"

"I don't know, I guessed it. She was like Marlene Dietrich singing 'Blowin' in the Wind,' the Dylan song, you know? Weird stuff, spooky, but very up-close and personal—it's hard to explain, but personal."

"So the Nazis take over the Earth and send ships in search of new worlds."

"Yes. In Thea von Harbou's version."

"And they find the Shadow. Isn't that a German story?"

"The story of the Shadow or the man who loses his shadow? I don't know."

"And it was Thea von Harbou who told you all this?"

"Johann believes that inhabited planets, or habitable planets, are the exception in the universe. . . . As he tells it, Guderian's tanks lay waste to Moscow . . ."

Boris Lejeune?"

"Yes."

The voice interrupts breakfast like a bomb, long anticipated but still capable of triggering surprise and terror. The caretaker jumps, drops his cup of tea, turns pale. Then he tries to stand, his feet tangling in the stool where he's sitting. On all fours, his gaze pleading, he crawls to where the tapes spin silently. He waits. He wonders, biting his lip, whether the voice that upset him just a moment ago was an auditory illusion. Finally, as if it were a prize for perseverance, though it isn't that at all, he hears a distant voice repeating a name from the speakers, which he has connected as quickly as he can. Cavalry Lieutenant Boris Lejeune. Then a laugh. Then static, magnified by the speakers, spills across the third floor of the academy, the second floor, the first floor, until it disappears into the yard, through which a girl is creeping. She's about seven years old, and her name is Carmen. Under her arm, she's carrying some tubes that she's "stolen" from the piles of junk in the grain shed. The noise stops her in midstride . . .

"And that's it?"

"What else did you expect?"

"The voice just says, I'm Lieutenant Boris Lejeune?"

"Cavalry Lieutenant."

"That's all?"

"There's a laugh. It's a boy's mocking, insolent laugh. 'Let me laugh for a second,' he says. 'As of now, I am Cavalry Lieutenant Boris Lejeune. The course will begin in a few minutes. This is new to me. Forgive me in advance for any errors. The uniform is nice-looking, true, but it's fucking cold out here. The course begins now. My regiment has set up camp next to a potato field.'"

"This voice from the dead comes as a complete surprise to the caretaker, I guess."

"Not exactly."

"And the girl is still standing there in the yard?"

"The girl, overcome by curiosity, opens the door a crack and looks in. There's no one on the first floor, of course, so she starts up the stairs, not bothering to be too careful."

"Meanwhile Boris Lejeune gazes out over a potato field."

"That's right. And as Lejeune is contemplating the field, the caretaker bustles around plugging and unplugging cables, starting tape recorders, jotting things down in a little notebook, testing the volume, et cetera. Vain and pointless tasks, nothing but testament to the fear that fills the old man now that the course, as the lieutenant said, has begun.

Meanwhile the girl has reached the third floor, and, hidden in the stairwell, she watches the whole scene with astonished eyes. The sky begins to brighten. Soon it exhibits a curious mix of whites and grays, an abundance of whimsical geometric figures. The only one who gazes pensively up at it is the cavalry lieutenant, as he's about to cross the potato field. The girl is too absorbed in the machines she's never seen before. The caretaker has eyes only for his connections. Lejeune sighs, then plants his officer's boots in the black soil and heads toward the tents erected on the far side of the potato field. In the camp, everything is a mess. When he passes the infirmary, Lejeune spies the first dead and stops whistling. A corporal points toward the staff officers' tents. As he moves that way, Lejeune realizes that they're breaking camp. But everything is being done so slowly that it's hard to tell whether the troops are setting up or tearing down. When at last he finds his superiors, Lejeune asks what he should do. Who are you? thunders the general. The girl, all at once, curls into a ball in the stairwell. The caretaker swallows. Lejeune answers: Lieutenant Boris Lejeune, I'm on the other side of the potato field, sir, I've just arrived. About time, says the general, and immediately forgets him. The conversation soon turns into an incomprehensible shouting match. Lejeune catches the words 'honor,' 'nation,' 'shame,' 'glory,' 'command,' et cetera, before sidling out of the tent. Now the girl smiles. The caretaker shakes his head as if to say, of course, I knew it. As the hours go by, a sense of defeat and panic grows in the encampment. Lejeune crosses back to the other side of the field and waits. Before night falls, a nervous hum rises from the camp. Some soldiers walking past yell: we're in a giant pocket! The Germans are going to fuck us good! Lejeune smiles and says: we've begun the course behind schedule, but here we go. Glory be, hip-hip hoorayayay! exclaims the caretaker. The girl backs away, suddenly realizing that it's night. An hour later, the gunfire begins."

Back then, for reasons unknown (though I could come up with a few), writing workshops were blossoming in Mexico City as never before. José Arco had some thoughts on the subject. It might be a scheme hatched from the beyond by the founding fathers, or an excess of zeal in some branch of the Education Department, or the visible manifestation of something else entirely, the sign of the Hurricane, as my friend explained, half serious and half joking. Whatever the case, the numbers told the story: according to the magazine *My Enchanted Garden,* whose publisher, editor in chief, and backer was the old poet and Michoacán politico Ubaldo Sánchez, in Mexico City alone the number of poetry journals of any size published in the year . . . was 125, by no means an inconsiderable sum, setting a record believed at the time to be unbreakable. Since then this torrent of magazines had been on the wane, until suddenly it began to wax again, from 32 in the previous year to 661 in the current year, and this proliferation, added Don Ubaldo, was by no means finished, since we were only in the month of . . . By the end of the year, he predicted a hair-raising total of one thousand poetry magazines, 90 percent of which would almost certainly cease to exist or undergo name changes and shifts in aesthetic tendencies in the year to come. How can it be, Don Ubaldo wondered, that in a city where illiteracy is growing by 0.5 percent annually, the production of poetry journals is on the rise? Likewise writing workshops, of which there were fifty-four in the previous year, according to the *Conasupo Cultural Weekly,* while in the current year the tally stands at two thousand. These figures, of course, have never been published in the bigger newspapers. And the fact that the *Conasupo Weekly* (which, as its name indicates, is a tabloid-size paper distributed to Conasupo employees along with three liters of milk) should attempt to document the number of workshops in Mexico City was suspicious in itself. José Arco and I tried to investigate further; or rather, he tried and I accompanied him, perched on the precarious rear seat of his Honda and getting to know the city along the way. The poet-editor of *My Enchanted Garden* lived in Colonia Mixcoac, in a big, ramshackle house on Calle Leonardo da Vinci. He welcomed us warmly, asked me what the hell I thought about what had just happened back where I was from, declared that the military was never to be trusted, then gave us some back issues of *My Enchanted Garden.* (It had been around for twenty-five years, if I remember correctly, and there were eighteen issues, some more polished than others and none more than fifteen pages long, from which Don

Ubaldo launched attacks on nearly every writer in Mexico.) As he went to get gin and a family-size bottle of Coca-Cola from the kitchen, he roared at us to be ready with our poems. With a little smile, José Arco chose one and put it on the table. What about you? asked Don Ubaldo. I'll send you something later, I lied. (When we left, I scolded my friend for his willingness to publish anywhere.) On our third drink, we asked him where he had come up with the figure of 661. We'd really like it if you could give us the names and addresses of all the magazines, said José Arco. Don Ubaldo looked at him with narrowed eyes. It was getting dark, and no light had been turned on. The question is offensive, boy, said the old man. After all these years of struggle, the name, at least, is familiar to them. Familiar to them? I asked. The publishers of these new journals, their distributors, they recognize the name of my journal, which was a pioneer in so many ways, as you have no way of knowing, of course, being new to the Republic. Sure, man, of course, said José Arco, but in your article you talk about a huge jump, and it's hard to believe that all those people have heard of *My Enchanted Garden,* isn't it? Don Ubaldo nodded slowly. Then he opened one of the drawers of his desk and took out a magazine printed on flimsy green paper, with type that seemed to leap from the page. There's something to what you say, son. Then he went on to explain that he had been sent 180 poetry journals this year, of which 25 dated to the previous year. Among the 155 new journals was the one we held in our hands. From it he had taken the information about the other 480 journals, which, together with *My Enchanted Garden,* accounted for the sum of 661. I can vouch for the truth of it; I've known Dr. Carvajal for a long time. Dr. Carvajal? The publisher of the journal you're holding in your hands, boys. The journal we were holding in our hands was called *Mexico and Its Arts,* and it was scarcely five pages long. The cover, a green sheet identical to the inner pages, featured the title, typewritten in capital letters (on an Olivetti Lettera 25, as Jan would later point out) and underlined twice; farther down, in parentheses and underlined just once, was *Poetry Bulletin of Mexico City;* at the bottom, not underlined, was the name of the publisher: Dr. Ireneo Carvajal. When we looked up, Don Ubaldo was smiling in satisfaction. The light that came in through the room's only window made him look like a stone gargoyle. The doctor is a poet? For the first time, José Arco began to show signs of hesitation, his voice barely audible in the darkness that was rapidly gaining ground. The creator of *My Enchanted Garden* chortled: no one had ever dared to call Dr. Carvajal a poet. Son of a bitch? Sure. Also: a nasty piece of work, a snake, a backstabbing recluse. Though he's read more than the three of us put together. Not without alarm, I noticed that as the evening went on, Ubaldo Sánchez had begun to look more and more like the Big Bad Wolf. The two of us must be turning into twin Little Red Riding Hoods, I thought. I turned the page: inside, there was a brief introductory note, followed by the names of the magazines and, sometimes, their addresses. On the back cover, the innocent phrase "Registration Pending" had a vague lapidary air. All at once, I felt that the little journal was burning my fingertips. Can I turn on the light, maestro? José Arco's voice was brusque. Don Ubaldo seemed to jump. Then he said something unintelligible and lumbered to his feet. The light, though weak, revealed a room where scattered papers and books seemed locked in combat. On a small table, I made out the cheap bust of an Indian warrior; on the walls, magazine pictures in black and white and color blended in with the wallpaper. Could you give us Dr. Carvajal's address? The old man nodded. All right, said José Arco, and I suppose we can keep this copy of the magazine? You suppose right, grumbled Don Ubaldo. As we were leaving, my eyes fell on a wrinkled sepia photograph on the desk: a group of soldiers on horseback, all but one gazing into the camera, and in the background a couple of 1920s Fords emerging from a great static dust cloud.

When he opened the door for us, it was starting to rain. I suppose you've noticed that this godforsaken city is hopping lately, hey, boys? Yes, said José Arco, we've noticed. Why is that? the old man whispered to himself.

In the next few days, I couldn't tag along with José Arco on his adventures, so when he turned up on our roof, Jan and I begged him to tell us what he'd discovered so far. Our friend's story was disappointing, but not without a hint of mystery. It went like this: A poet, promoter of the journal *The Flying North* (included, as it happens, in Dr. Ireneo Carvajal's report), and employee of Conasupo, where he occupied some obscure post—doorman, office boy, or typist, I can't remember—had so far been his only source of information. From this poet, he learned that the *Weekly* was hardly ever distributed among the administrative staff but that it could be found on any counter of the chain of cheap Conasupo supermarkets around Mexico City. Though "any counter" was an exaggeration, as my friend soon realized: there were supermarkets where the *Weekly* had never been seen and others where the employees, after digging through piles of papers, managed to retrieve five- or six-month-old issues. In total, José Arco collected four *Cultural Weekly*s, counting the one he already had when he began the search. The poet from *The Flying North* thought that the publisher and editor of the *Weekly* was someone from the cultural department, and, unfortunately for us, he didn't know anyone there. Given the quality of the print job and the paper, it seemed evident that the *Weekly* was well funded. There was no point discussing why it was distributed in supermarkets; the way things were done at the hypothetical cultural department must be the same way things were done at offices everywhere. Here José Arco's friend insisted on the possible nonexistence of the department in question. So it was fruitless to seek explanations. The conversation ended with an invitation for us to send unpublished work to *The Flying North*. Then José Arco, on his Honda, made the rounds of ten or fifteen cheap supermarkets, and, in the end, not sure exactly why he was wasting his time, he found himself in possession of four *Weekly*s. Leaving aside the one we'd read already, the remaining three were devoted to (1) urban *corridos;* (2) poetesses (Mexican or foreign) in Mexico City (including an incredible number of women whose names, not to mention whose work, we had never heard of); and (3) graffiti in Mexico City—invisible art or decadent art? And that was all, for now. José Arco believed that somehow—he would come up with a way soon—he would meet the author or authors of the *Weekly,* whose articles, it goes without saying, were always published anonymously. What kind of person could it be? A true avant-gardist, a CIA agent—whatever, stranger things had been seen at Conasupo. And naturally he was still trying to land an interview with Dr. Carvajal.

"Maybe they're the same person," I suggested.

"Possibly, but I doubt it."

"What I'd like to know is how you got the first *Weekly,* the one about the poetry workshops, though actually the issues with the poetesses and the graffiti are the best," said Jan.

"It's a funny thing," said José Arco. "I got it from Estrellita. You'll have to meet her soon."

"Estrellita?"

"The spirit of La Habana," said José Arco.

Dear Robert Silverberg:

Are you on the North American Committee of Science Fiction Writers in Support of the Third World's Neediest Cases? If not, here's my suggestion: join up, affiliate yourself, form subcommittees in San Diego, Los Angeles, Seattle, Oakland, at universities where you're booked as a speaker, at bars in three-star hotels. If your body still has the energy that you've poured into your work, become part of the committee and rev it up. Pretend that this is your blind twin sister speaking to you, and trust me. I see you as capable, you and a few others, of gazing into the liquid eyes of the essence of the committee and not running away howling like a madman. And as your blind twin, I say to you: onward, Robert, prove not only that after a long (very long) journey you've learned to write like the common man; prove that the North American Committee of Science Fiction Writers in

Support of the Third World's Neediest Cases can count
on your help. Donald Wollheim would have joined. Who
knows, maybe even Professor Sagan, in his worst
nightmares. (On second thought, not Donald Wollheim.)
But it's your turn now, and you can bring along your
writer friends, brighten the day of the secretary-general,
who sits alone and bored in a dreary little room in San
Francisco. Call him on the phone, let the black phone
ring and the trembling hand lift the receiver. Is Harlan
Ellison on the case? Is Philip José Farmer on the case, or
is he masturbating up on the roof? Go to work for the
committee before the spiral stairs vanish—first in sleep
and then into nothingness—on their way up to the best
roofs. Empty room, dirty windows, frayed rugs, a
glass of whiskey on the table, a clock, a rumpled
cushion—none of this does any good. The scene, my
dear Robert, is this: dog-colored dawn, spaceships
appear over the mountains on the horizon, Chile goes
down along with the rest of Latin America, we become
fugitives, you become killers. And the image isn't a still,
it isn't "forever," it isn't some stiff heroic dream; it's
moving—in multiple directions!—and those who tangle
tomorrow as fugitives and killers might the day after
tomorrow shove their faces together into the void,
yes? Parts of what you've written, I've enjoyed so
much. . . . I'd really like it if we could manage to stay
alive and meet. . . . Cross the line . . . No barriers . . .

And pretend that we believe that the committee's Eye
of Stone is one of Pepito Farmer's jokes . . . Wonderful!
All my love!

Yours,
Jan Schrella

Amid the gunfire and confusion, Lejeune makes his escape with a colonel and a Parisian recruit. What's your opinion of all this, Colonel? Lejeune asks as he runs. The colonel won't or can't answer, so our lieutenant addresses the same question to the Paris recruit. A fucking mess. It's all the officers' fault—they screwed us, says the recruit. Shut up and run, orders the colonel. At last the three of them stop on a ridge, watching as the tanks go by and a column of prisoners forms in the German rear guard. The colonel, exhausted, gets out a cigarette, lights it, inhales a few times, and finally points the smoldering tip at the recruit: you should be ashamed of what you just said. I swear I'll have you court-martialed for insubordination and disrespect. The recruit shrugs. I swear it, says the colonel, I'll have our own soldiers shoot you, or the Germans, I don't care. What's your opinion of all this, and what are you going to do? Lejeune asks the recruit. The latter considers for a few seconds, then turns, points his gun at the colonel's chest, and fires. Lejeune poses the first part of the question again. The recruit says he has no idea, that this won't be over anytime soon. The colonel's body twitches on the dark grass. Lejeune leans over and asks what he believes is the best defense against the enemy. Order, says the colonel, ashen-faced. Then he says, my God, my God, and dies. The column of prisoners begins to move. The recruit empties the colonel's pockets, taking his cigarettes, his money, and his watch, and heads down the ridge to join the prisoners. Lejeune sits on the ground. Next to the dead man's body is a photograph of a woman, with 'Monique and the breeze. St. Cyr' written on the back. He stares at the woman for a long time. She's young and pretty. When he has looked for long enough, he lies down on his back and stares up at the stars that swell in the vault of the heavens. At this point the academy caretaker remembers that Huachofeo describes a similar scene in his *Paradoxical History of Latin America*."

"What about the girl?"

"The girl has gone down the stairs without a sound, exited the grain shed, gone home, eaten a plate of beans left for her on the table, taken off her shoes, and gotten into bed with her mother. The caretaker has eaten a hard-boiled egg, drank a cup of tea, and lain down on a mat, covering himself with a couple of vicuña blankets. Lieutenant Boris Lejeune has fallen asleep gazing up at the stars."

"Do they dream about the Hurricane?"

"Maybe. The next morning, Lejeune is in constant motion: he has his picture taken with General Gamelin,

General Giraud, General de Gaulle, General Weygand, General Blanchard, General Gort's chief of staff, gazing out over Arras or Ypres, on the streets of Lille, Givet, Sedan, or on the banks of the Meuse and the dunes of Dunkirk. Meanwhile the caretaker follows his usual morning routine in every particular: he has a quick, frugal breakfast and gets straight to work. The girl wakes with a fever. Her dreams were about a nuclear blast, I think, a Yankee battalion wiping out Los Ángeles with a couple of neutron bombs. On the banks of the Bío-Bío is the Hurricane, and when the bombs explode, the Hurricane opens up like a giant cinema, and inside is a factory called Pompeya, where motorcycles are built. Benelli motorcycles. Soon a motorcycle emerges from the factory, and then another and another: a battalion of Komsomols from the south of Chile on its way to destroy or be destroyed by the Yankees. Then it begins to dawn on the caretaker that all the pieces of the course have almost reached Santa Bárbara, or at least they're on their way. The girl's mother brings down her daughter's fever with paper-thin slices of raw potato soaked in vinegar. Boris Lejeune has himself photographed in a French tank on the outskirts of Abbeville."

Hmm, said José Arco, a match in his hand, so that's the guy's signature, a triangle with a mouth in it. I lit another match. What happened to the fucking light? It's been out for two days. Look, this is what I was telling you about. I moved a little closer. The smell of shit and urine rose from the sticky floor. This is it? Yes, said José Arco, lighting another match. I can't see a thing. So that's supposed to be a cave? Come closer, I'm going to light two matches; you light two and then look. In the glow of the four little tongues of flame, I saw the cross-hatched outline of a cave, some of the lines very bold, others barely visible on the white tile. In fact, it looked less like a cave than like a doughnut hacked with an ax. Inside the doughnut, it was possible to make out the silhouettes or shadows of two human beings, a dog shitting, and a mushroom cloud. Well, can you see it now? I nodded. Plain enough, isn't it? Terrifying, I replied. The dog has three tails, did you notice? Yes, of course, he's wagging his tail. And shitting at the same time? Of course. Shitting

63

and wagging his tail. And what are the people doing? I don't know, the first time I saw it, I thought that they were holding hands, but now I'm not sure. Anyway, look closer, I think they're shadows, not bodies. The shadows from Plato's cave? Whoa, I wouldn't bet on that, but there's something about the size of the mushroom cloud that makes me want to call them shadows. So they're looking at us, and we see their shadows reflected on the wall of the cave? No, they have their backs to us, they're looking out the mouth of the cave because on the horizon, far away, an atomic bomb has exploded. Maybe. And the dog? Why is the dog shitting in the cave? Heh-heh. Touching detail, isn't it? No, I think he's shitting because he's scared, poor Rin-Tin-Tin. When they're scared, they don't wag their tails. I had a dog when I was a boy, and I can tell you that for a fact. I've never had a dog, you know? Now that I think about it, I'm pretty sure you're the first person I ever knew who had a dog. Give me a break. Shhh, careful, someone's coming. I closed the door to the stall. A second later, we heard the click of a switch and then the sound of liquid splashing on the urinal outside. An instant later, whoever it was zipped up and left. The matches had gone out, and I realized that I had burned my thumb and index finger. José Arco lit another match. It's a weird signature, he said, unfazed. A triangle with a fat-lipped mouth in it, in midshout—that's what it looks like. Probably inspired by the Stones logo, but a savage cubist version of it. Fine, I said. I saw it, now let's get out of here. Did you examine it carefully? I don't know, I said, this place makes me dizzy. I wonder whether it was the artist himself who made the bulb burn out, murmured José Arco. When we emerged, the lights of the café dazzled us and seemed to speed up our movements. We couldn't help it, it was if we were dancing around the tables back to the spot where we had left our coffees.

All of these episodes José Arco dubbed "the Investigation." Basically, we were just trying to confirm the reports from the *Conasupo Cultural Weekly* and Dr. Carvajal's journal, and following any clues that cropped up along the way. Soon we were visiting all kinds of poetry workshops and we had gotten our hands on journals whose sole print runs were often no more than ten xeroxed copies. We also remained on the lookout for the graffiti—invisible art or decadent art?— described in the *Weekly*. Luck was clearly on our side, since it soon brought several of our working hypotheses together in one place. This place was Café La Habana, where José Arco found the Triangle with a Mouth (or Laughing Triangle) graffiti. It was an establishment already frequented by my friend in the days before the start of the Investigation, if not as assiduously. One random evening at La Habana, as he was talking to a group of friends, Estrellita asked him to buy her a coffee, and then she gave him the *Weekly*. Gave it to him, nobody else. Days later, after searching for her in vain along Bucareli, he found the drawing of the cave in the toilet stall. And so, over the days that followed, as we searched for Estrellita (halfheartedly, I must add), La Habana became the main headquarters of our meanderings, and then, in the most natural way, it was the place we washed up after eleven each night. We discovered that the block of Bucareli between La Habana and the Reloj Chino wasn't just a kind of shrine—something we intuited that we should keep in mind—but that it more than satisfied all our alimentary needs: on one corner, there was a sandwich stand run by an ex–Atlante footballer, and on the other corner was La Habana, which served the cheapest and most delicious chilaquiles on the block; in between was an extremely cheap pizza counter owned by an American guy with a Mexican wife, a guy everybody called Jerry Lewis even though he looked nothing at all like the actor; across the street was a taco-and-quesadilla stand run by two dark-skinned sisters who, the minute they saw me, would say, *¿Qué pasó, güero?* and I would say, but I'm not a white boy, and they would say, what do you mean you're not, and me, stubborn, *no soy güero,* and so on until José Arco arrived and put an end to it: *¿Güero?* Of course you are; and working both sides of the street was a gay one-eyed vendor of elotes, tender corncobs spread with butter or mayonnaise or crema and dusted with cheese or chile powder, who sagely recommended the Bucareli movie theater as the ideal place to eat his merchandise. The Bucareli theater was the king of the block, no question about it, a benevolent king, practically a paragon of virtue, host of those with nowhere to sleep, dark Disneyland, the only church that, at times, we seemed destined to belong to.

And then we found Estrellita.

José Arco pointed at a table. There she was, sitting up

very straight, with two girls. The one on the left is Teresa, said my friend with a hint of bitterness. And the other one? Ah, that's Angélica Torrente, let's go somewhere else. What do you mean? I burst out. There's Estrellita, we've been looking for her like crazy, and now we're going to leave? Forget it! José Arco didn't answer. As I was shaking him, I watched the three women through the window out of the corner of my eye. Estrellita was very old, and her long face was covered in wrinkles. She hadn't taken off her coat. She was drinking something, and every so often her face turned toward one or the other of her companions, a permanent smile fixed on it. The two girls were talking and laughing and, maybe by contrast, seemed incredibly young. And smart, shielded by the same yellow light of the café that fell over them like a curtain or a dome—super smart and super pretty, I thought.

At last we went in, though I almost had to drag José Arco. Estrellita scarcely noticed our presence at the table. Teresa and Angélica Torrente, however, didn't seem pleased to have to suddenly change the subject. José Arco, embarrassed (my friend, I realized then, was excruciatingly shy around girls he liked), introduced me in a way that was clearly an apology for the intrusion. Hello, I said. José Arco coughed and asked what time it was. Before he could escape, I pulled up two chairs, and we sat down.

"So you're Teresa." The look on José Arco's face was more agonized than withering. "The other day, we left the motorcycle outside your place, did you see it?"

"Yes." Teresa—another discovery—could be ice-cold, though she was only nineteen or twenty.

Angélica Torrente seemed friendlier and nicer.

"Where the hell did you come from?" she asked.

"Me? . . . From Chile . . ."

The two of them laughed. Estrellita's beatific smile deepened slightly. I smiled. Ha-ha. Yes, I'm from Chile. Angélica Torrente was seventeen, and she had won the Eloísa Ramírez Prize for young poets. (Eloísa Ramírez had died fifteen years ago, before she turned eighteen, leaving behind a giant stack of papers and a pair of inconsolable parents who, in her memory, awarded a not-insignificant annual cash prize for the best collection of poetry by a writer under twenty or twenty-one or something like that.) Angélica Torrente's charms were electric, mainly, and a touch acidic. She talked like a person on the crest of a wave; she could see everything from up there, though she didn't pay much attention to the sights because of the speed and the falling. She was definitely very beautiful, sometimes even painfully so. She had a laugh—unusual for her age—that was the thing you remembered most about her when she dumped you in the end; it was her signature, her trademark, her weapon. She laughed easily, an open, happy laugh, and the combination of the sound and the way she moved hinted at dark dreams, paranoia, the urge to live life to the hilt whether or not you ended up battered and bruised. Teresa was different: not only did she seem more serious, sometimes she actually was. She was a poetess, too, though unlike Angélica and the others I would soon meet, Teresa worked. She was a typist, and she was studying medicine, in her second semester. She didn't live with her parents. She was beginning to make a name for herself in some journals—not many of them, but good ones—as someone not to be overlooked when anthologies of young Mexican poets were assembled. Her relationship with José Arco, despite appearances, was completely atypical. I never knew, and never asked, whether they had slept together. Maybe they had, maybe they hadn't. I don't think it matters. It's common knowledge that Teresa came to hate José Arco, which I presume means that at some point she loved him. There's one thing that tells you all you need to know about Teresa: she would never lend you a book, and if you made the mistake of loaning her one—as José Arco did a thousand times at least—you could bet anything that you would never see it again, or if you did, it would be in her bookcase, blond wood with mahogany streaks and knots, very pretty, very elegant. Between the two girls, Estrellita was like a grain of sand in a saucer of coffee.

"We've been looking for you, Estrellita," said José Arco.

Estrellita sighed. Then she said "hmm," gazing past my friend's forehead, and she sighed again, putting everything into her smile.

"We've been looking for you because of the *Weekly* you gave me the other day."

"Hmm?"

"Do you remember? The *Conasupo Cultural Weekly,* about the poetry workshops . . ."

"Ah? Hmm . . ." Estrellita studied a point in the distance and huddled into her coat.

"Do you remember it? A long list of poetry workshops, Mexico City poetry workshops."

"What are you talking about?" asked Angélica.

"A really weird magazine, maybe a conspiracy," I said.

"Oh, yes . . ." said Estrellita. "Did you like it?"

"Very much."

"Oh, I'm glad . . ."

"I'd like to know where you got it. . . . Who gave it to you?"

Estrellita smiled. There wasn't a single tooth in her mouth.

"Hmm, it's a strange story, a lovely one . . ."

"Tell us," said José Arco and Teresa.

But the old woman sat there unmoving, her pale green eyes fixed on the tabletop. We waited. The sounds of La Habana, dwindling at this time of night, wrapped around us like Estrellita's threadbare coat. It was nice. Now Angélica Torrente showed herself to be the most practical of us all.

"Do you want another coffee?"

"Yes."

Not many knew exactly who Estrellita was. She turned up in the most unexpected places, like a battered reproduction of the Angel of Independence or Liberty Leading the People. No one knew where she lived—though theories were ventured—or even if Estrellita was really her name. When asked, she would sometimes say that it was Carmen, or Adela, or Evita, but she also claimed that Estrella was her real name and not, as was commonly believed, the pet name given to her by some old man from Spain who had killed himself. At La Habana, it was assumed that she was a poet, though as far as I know, no one, or hardly anyone, had read anything she wrote. According to her, rivers and rivers of ink—seas of ink—had flowed since she published her last sonnet. She had a son. The old reporters who hung around La Habana didn't know much about art, but they swore that he had been a good painter. In fact, Estrellita's only visible source of income was a set of prints made from her son's drawings, which she sold from table to table. It was said that heroin had ended his career but that he was still alive, and here came the saddest part: he was living with his mother. The drawings were wild, reminiscent of Leonora Carrington: spiderwebs, moons, bearded women, dwarfs—bad, essentially. There must have been about twenty of them, maybe fewer, copied a thousand times over, because Estrellita really did sell them and she never ran out. Who had ordered so many prints? The son himself? Judging from the paper, they had been printed at least fifteen years ago. Estrellita considered them a blessing, and maybe they were: she supported herself and her son—who was in his forties now—on the proceeds, tucking sweet rolls for him into the deep pockets of her coat and nourishing herself on milky coffee in tall glasses with a long spoon so that she could reach the bottom without wetting her fingers, font of energy.

"Don't burn yourself," said Angélica.

Estrellita sipped, tasting, then put in enough sugar for three glasses.

"Hmm, delicious," she said.

"Do you like it very sweet?" asked Angélica.

"Yes."

"Estrellita, are you going to tell us where you got the *Weekly*?"

"Yes, yes . . ."

"Where?"

"At a supermarket . . ."

José Arco opened his eyes and smiled.

"Of course," he said. "I'm an idiot."

"I went in to buy a princess dress . . ."

". . ."

"And a yogurt . . ."

". . ."

"And they gave me this paper, for free . . ."

"Thank you, Estrellita," said my friend.

"Are you doing anything tonight?" asked Angélica Torrente half an hour later, informed of all the dumb things—according to her—that we'd been doing.

"No," I said.

"There's a kind of party at my place. Do you want to come?"

"I'd love to," I said.

Dear Fritz Leiber:

I think you must know this story. Like love at first sight, without the love, comes the True Encounter; every organ in the body transmitting and receiving; organic radar units shuffling along the last streets of a Latin American city, drinking and taking peso buses, winking at the void. At the other end of the bar, the anthropoid suddenly discovers that the stranger, too, is interested in the figures sketched on the wall. After that, everything moves even more slowly, if possible; a montage of aquatic scenes of two characters who meet in unexpected places; washrooms in fleabag movie theaters, cantinas frozen in 1940, underground clubs, the Chapultepec roller coaster, dark and deserted parks. And then there is the only repeated scene: the first and last meeting of the terrestrial explorer and the alien takes place in the inner courtyard of a *pulquería*. Upon exiting through the wrong door, the earth dweller comes across the alien

vomiting in a corner. Calmly, he raises his video camera
and records the scene. What the alien registers is not the
barely perceptible hum of the camera but the presence of
something that he has been obscurely pursuing for
centuries. When he turns, the moon disappears behind
the rooftops. The owner of the establishment says she
heard shouts, splashing, curses, singing. Real nice guys,
a couple of sympathetic empaths, was how she put it.
That night, she found bloodstains on the dirt floor of the
courtyard. This is the source of the legend that once a
year, in mid-February, the tourist and the local still do
battle in the sky. The truth, I think, is that they both died
that night. Is there any American university that might
put up money for a team to search for clues to this
Mystery? Some private foundation, maybe? It's a true
story, and I'm afraid that it's prophetic. It's in our mutual
interest, etc., etc., for our mutual survival, etc., etc.

Much love and thanks,
Jan Schrella

Seriously, now, let's talk about your book—your monumental work."

"My work, as you call it, begins on the third floor of the Potato Academy, in old Santa Bárbara, in the foothills of the Andes. It's the story of Boris, son of Juan Gonzales and student aide at the Unknown University. An ordinary kid."

"Wait. There's some interruption. Do you hear a strange noise?"

"It must be those alcoholics yelling. Who would've thought renowned intellectuals and men of letters (God shit on them) could make such a racket? Even the ones who've fallen asleep are snoring like bears."

"They're celebrating your triumph, my young friend."

"Look at that old man: he's got his face in his wife's crotch."

"That's not his wife. Never mind. All his life he's fought for the perfect word and silence. Otherness. Now he's scared but happy. The reason for his happiness is you. You and your magnificent poems."

"I get the sense that the only sober person in this Republic of Letters bacchanal is me. You, dear reporter, have had a touch too much vodka. It's clear that I'm not here for my 'magnificent' poems."

"Anyway, back to your work. How is the girl? Is she still sick?"

"No. Now there's a fiesta in town, and the girl walks the streets with a crown of flowers in her hair. The people gather in the Plaza de Armas, and then they stream along the streets of town. They're singing as they go. There aren't many of them, as I've said. The town isn't big, and the song that they sing has no words: it's a string of aa-ohh, aa-ohh, ee-ahh, ee-ahh sounds, a little like an Indian lament."

"At a certain point, they pass in front of the Potato Academy."

"Yes. The caretaker is watching from the window. The procession continues to the end of Calle Galvarino, turns onto Valdivia, and is gone. Only the girl is left standing in the middle of the street, and this time the caretaker notices her. The sky, of course, suddenly grows dark."

"Does the girl think it's a haunted house?"

"No. She's still too little for that. In fact, she hesitates for a second and goes into the academy. From the window, the caretaker sees her shadow flit across the yard, and then he hears her light step on the stairs. The old man softens. Ah, he thinks, ah. The bride. The betrothed. The eyes that could look upon Boris with love. The immaculate child on her way up the stairs, believing herself unseen. Then, of course, he goes back to his cables and reels. He has time; the broadcast isn't for a while yet. The electric bill for the grain shed at 800 Galvarino is the highest in Santa Bárbara. If he gets raided someday, that might be why. I think it was Dan Mitrione who, back in the day, taught the cops how to hunt leftists by reading the electric meter. Any house that uses too much or too little electricity is suspicious. The crowd, meanwhile, returns to the plaza after making a loop around town, and now they begin to disperse. Silence descends on the streets once again. A silence for which the caretaker is grateful: he can handle interruptions and curious girls, but not this revelry and celebration, painful because they remind him of his sad life devoted to his work. But let's not exaggerate. The caretaker gets intoxicated and dances, too, in his own way. His holidays are pure potential. He doesn't know what boredom is. The recipe for spicy potato cake is his exclusive property. Nothing to sniff at, wouldn't you agree?"

"It must be a sad life—yours, I mean, my young friend."

"Sure: I've squandered my adolescence in seedy movie theaters and pestilent libraries. To make matters worse, my girlfriends always leave me."

"Now everything might change. A bright future lies ahead of you."

"Do you say that because of the prize?"

"Because of everything that the prize entails."

"You poor, naïve reporter. First you mistake this room in the middle of some random forest for a crystal palace on a hill. Then you actually predict a bright future for art. You don't realize yet that this is a trap. Who the hell do you think I am, Sid Vicious?"

Everything that happened at Angélica Torrente's house, as I remember it, fades into the background, as a prelude to the loud ring of the bell. Someone's at the door, and everyone's in Lola Torrente's room, and I go to answer it, the door: coming!

But there are things that I remember vividly—books, records (the shiny black objects themselves, I mean, not the music), and, especially, Lola Torrente, two years older than Angélica, much darker, bigger-boned, not thin at all. To me, her smile is still the terminal smile of that other Mexico, a place sometimes revealed between the folds of a random dawn: part rabid will to live, part sacrifice stone. It's not too much to say that for an hour I had been in love with Angélica. Or that around midnight, more or less, my love gradually faded until it perished entirely, amid glasses of alcohol and cigarettes and don't touch Mallarmé, assholes, you'll fuck it up. It's possible that the rapid rise and fall of this great platonic love had something to do with Lola Torrente. I don't mean—this would be the height of fickleness—that during the course of the party I transferred my affections from one sister to the other, but rather that first (let's be honest), Angélica wouldn't give me the time of day, and second, as the only person there who didn't know everyone, I was limited to the role of observer (though unfortunately I did open my mouth, too), and at some point that was how I discovered that there was a structure of mirrors between the two sisters, mirrors in which each of them was distorted and reflected back at the other like a message, so that one sister might receive a still and harmless figure and the other a little glass ball under the bed, though most of the time they were firing deadly laser beams back and forth. The star of the party and of everything was Angélica. The powerful shadow was Lola. And it was this and the certainty with which Angélica handled the situation (but especially, as I've said, her manifest indifference to me) that left me on the sidelines, relegated to the joys of the observer. Anyway, Angélica wasn't lacking in suitors; neither, I must admit, was Lola, though her suitors (actually just one suitor, but a nice one) were nothing like the promises made flesh who courted her sister. The issue, according to Pepe Colina, a Nicaraguan versed in Horace and Virgil, was that Angélica was a virgin and Lola wasn't, and at least one or two hundred people knew it. I glared at him—some things are simply in bad taste—and then I asked him how two hundred people could be aware of such an intimate detail. From people like me, of course, he replied. I guessed, not without blushing, that

Pepe Colina had slept with Lola Torrente. An odd couple, I thought, in the tradition of the short, glasses-wearing guy and the strong, independent woman. I lit a Delicado, feigning indifference. I felt myself getting an erection. I retreated to the bathroom and finished smoking the cigarette. At a certain point, I looked at myself in the mirror and started to laugh very softly. On my way out, I almost ran into Lola Torrente. She was a little bit drunk. Her eyes were dark and bright. She whispered something unintelligible, smiling, and closed the door. I knew that our friendship had been sealed.

I went back to the living room, literally bouncing with joy. What was José Arco doing meanwhile? Surrounded by the shyest, least graceful, and worst dancers, my friend was telling stories: the new Peruvian poetry, the Hora Zero group, Martín Adán's silver knife, Oquendo de Amat, and other stories, too, new to young Mexican poets back then, stories as true and horrifying as life itself, in which his Honda scaled the highways and trails of western Mexico until it reached an eagle's crag of toughness, what Baldomero Lillo called the very center of the hot potato, whereupon he launched himself at 120 or 130 kilometers an hour along the twisting path of the story.

That night's tale was inspired by a prolonged absence from Mexico City, or something like that, not that it matters. It begins with José Arco arriving at a solitary beach where he finds nothing but a single dog. No fishermen, no houses, nothing—just the motorcycle, José Arco, and the dog. The rest is paradise, and in the sand my friend writes *mi mamá me mima* and all the other first words. He lives on cans of condensed milk and tuna. The dog is always with him. One afternoon, a ship appears. José Arco rides up the cliff on his motorcycle (in his telling, the black Honda will go wherever you want it to go if your heart is pure); the dog comes along, too. The people on the ship see him and wave. José Arco waves back. We're from Greenpeace! they shout. *Ay,* whispers José Arco. What are you doing there, where are you from, who are you, how did you get that motorcycle up there, is there a road? Their questions are left unanswered. The captain announces that he's coming over. José Arco and the captain meet on the beach. As they're about to shake hands, the dog attacks the eco-skipper. The crew members who came over with the captain rush to his defense, kicking the dog and then roughing up José Arco. Five against one and a dog. Then they patch him up, put Merthiolate on him and the dog, apologize, advise him to keep the mutt tied up. Before it gets dark, they return to the ship and sail off. José Arco, bruised and battered, watches them go from under a palm tree, his dog at his feet and his motorcycle nearby. The captain and the young men and women of the crew wave to him from the horizon. The dog whimpers, and so does my friend, but then, as the ship is about to vanish from sight, he leaps on the motorcycle and roars up to the top of the cliff. Behind him comes the dog, limping a little, and they watch the ship as it sails away.

Teresa: I'll die before you get me to believe that.

Angélica: What did you do next?

Pepe Colina (lighting a joint and passing it to Angélica): Man, the only decent eco-skipper there ever was or ever will be was Captain Ahab, a truly misunderstood man.

Regina Castro (poetess, thirty, as yet unpublished, purveyor of birth-control pills to her younger peers, decent writer but nothing special): Tell me—what happened to the dog?

Lola: And what is Greenpeace?

Héctor Gómez (in love with Lola Torrente, twenty-seven, La Habana regular, elementary-school teacher): A pacifist movement, Lola . . . To be honest, Pepe, I find it hard to believe what you're telling us.

José Arco: Don't call me Pepe.

Teresa (smiling at Héctor Gómez, who pours more vodka): Well, of course it's a complete lie. José doesn't like the beach, and there's no way he could spend three days in a row in a place where there weren't any people.

José Arco: Well, I was there.

Two Lit. Dept. students: We believe you, poet.

Regina Castro: What about the dog? Did you bring it back with you?

José Arco: No, it got left there.

Pepe Colina: Or Jonah, if we can call him a sailor. An eco-friendly guy, for sure, like everybody back then, but it might be a stretch to call him a skipper . . .

Angélica: He didn't follow you? Strange.

Antonio Mendoza (bard of the proletariat, twenty, proofreader at a government agency): The thing is, José doesn't have room for another dog.

Angélica (giving Antonio a tender look): What?

Antonio Mendoza: There's no room at home for another dog.

Lola: I didn't know you had one already.

Angélica: Who's the dog, Antonio?

Antonio Mendoza: Me. Sometimes.

José Arco: What the fuck are you talking about?

Antonio Mendoza: And him sometimes.

Pepe Colina: Uh-huh, totally wasted. (He laughs.) They're children. Unless it's some kind of joke, man, but a fucked-up joke like that is bad news.

Héctor Gómez (to Lola): How about we get some fresh air?

Pepe Colina (when Héctor and Lola are gone): We should all get some fresh air . . .

Antonio Mendoza (relaxed all of a sudden): They went to fuck in the yard . . .

Teresa: Could you shut up for once, idiot?

Antonio Mendoza: Are you jealous?

Teresa: Me? You're drunk . . .

Two Lit. Dept. students: Bottles that haven't been opened yet . . . Joy, joy . . .

Angélica: No more drinking here!

Antonio Mendoza (putting a hand on her waist): Hey, Angélica . . .

Angélica: And don't touch my sister!

Antonio Mendoza: But I never—

Regina Castro (commandingly and without raising her voice): Shut up for a change and sit down. I was going to read a poem, but the way you're all acting . . .

Teresa: Oh, please, read it.

Pepe Colina: Madame Poetess, I'm all ears.

Two Lit. Dept. students (pouring drinks for those present): Wait until we're all ready.

Estrellita (her head popping around the kitchen door): Oh, a reading, lovely . . .

I couldn't stand it, and I fled onto the balcony. The poem threatened to be uncommonly long: Regina Castro's childhood and adolescence in San Luis Potosí, her family, her dolls, her Catholic school, recess, her Carrancista grandfather, the rocking chair, the dresses, the trunks, the cellar, Regina's lips, her older sister's lips, high heels, the poetry of López Velarde. Meanwhile it was a clear night, and the lights in the other apartments hinted at parties five meters above our heads, leisurely conversations five meters below our feet, maybe a couple of old men listening to classical music fifteen meters in a straight line from our ribs. I was happy. It didn't seem very late, but even if every light went out and all that was left was me and the glow of my cigarette suspended on the wonderful balcony, this particular beauty or terrible fleeting calm wouldn't melt away. The moon seemed to creak over reality. Behind me, through the bulk of the building, I heard the whisper of traffic. Sometimes, if I was quiet, holding my cigarette motionless in the air, I could hear the click of the lights changing and then another click or, more precisely, a *rhrrr,* and the long cars moved on down Avenida Universidad. Three floors below, the gravel yard and the building's garden were connected by narrow paths of black dirt bordering big trees and planters. From the balcony, the garden looked like a capital B on its side, like this Ɑ. Inside one of the semicircles, there was an open space, slanted like a Chinese eye, with three benches, two swing sets, and a seesaw, presided over by a good-size stone, probably a sculpture. Winding around behind this space was a sinuous black line, maybe a ditch, and two feet beyond it rose the wall separating the building from its neighbor. There, against the wall, in a space behind the bushes hidden to passersby but visible from the exact spot on the balcony where I was standing, Lola Torrente brought Héctor Gómez's cock to her mouth and began to suck it, as if she had been waiting for me.

But this was no ordinary blow job: shrine suddenly alight, soon all that existed were Lola's hands, one around Hector's penis, the other between his legs, and Héctor's fingers buried in her hair—her beautiful, strong head of black hair—and Lola's mouth and shoulders and knees on the black grass or black earth or shadow, and the smiles that weren't smiles, every so often discreetly directed at each other.

This, without a doubt, was secret Balinese theater.

Only when I went back into the living room did a single shudder run through me.

There was no one in the room.

I think I drank something and sat down. I picked up a book from the table. From one of the rooms came voices, maybe the start of an argument. Then I heard laughter, nothing serious. I closed my eyes: sounds barely audible on the ghost channel. I remembered what Jan said about Boris. I had never believed him. It's true, said Jan. You'll go crazy, I said. No, no, no, no. Jungle, I thought, out there is the jungle. Boris was what, fifteen? No, no, no. I got up and went into the kitchen.

I'm always amazed by refrigerators full of food.

I went back to the living room with a glass of milk and sat down, sipping it slowly. I must have looked ridiculous there with my legs crossed and tears in my eyes. But why? Jan's voice droned on in the background of the Balinese theater. I've told you a thousand times, Remo, and you still don't get it. Fateful figures in an incomprehensible game of chess. All I can see, I said, is the silhouette of a boy . . . dancing in a room. He must be happy. A boy of thirteen dancing in his bedroom. Now he's turning, and I can see his face, Boris's face? And then the room is plunged into darkness, the power is out all over the neighborhood, and all I hear is the sound of his breathing, the sound of his body dancing in silence. I set the glass on a night table. The leg that was crossed over my knee began to jerk as if the Invisible Doctor was checking my reflexes with his little steel hammer. Stop, I said, quiet, come on, Rinti, stop, hee-hee, good boy.

Then came that famous ring at the door, *dingdong, ringgg, ttlililinggg*, I swear I can't remember the tones, *screeekkkkk, brrrrringggg, lingalingaling,* and I jumped up because I sensed or guessed, *ronngggdronnggg,* that from here to total happiness, *ping ping-ping, hhhwhishh,* there were just one or two or three million steps, and I set out on the path by making my way to the door, *deet-deet-deet,* which I opened. It was a girl with brown hair. Behind her: a very disagreeable—and very ugly—boy with hair the same color.

Dear Ursula K. Le Guin:

What can we, the creechies, do when the hour comes?
Is our weapon our crushing majority? Is our weapon the
ability to see our aggressor as a snake? Is our weapon our
capacity to translate the word "death"? Is our weapon our
Blind Deaf Mute Faith in survival? Is our weapon
audacity? Are our weapons our arrows that fly up toward
the helicopters like a dream or like the scattered
fragments of a dream? Is our weapon implacability? Are
our weapons the Dorados who ride drunk and never stop
shooting at the column of tanks? An old Agustín Lara
record on the exact border of nothing? Flying saucers
that land in the Andes and take off from the Andes? Our
creechie identity? The art of swift communication? The
art of camouflage? Our explosive anal fixation? Pure
fierceness? What will be given to us, and what must we
seize in order to fight and triumph? Should we stop
gazing at the moon forever and ever? Learn once and for

all to stop Guderian's tanks at the gates of Moscow? Who should we wake with a kiss and break the spell? Madness or Beauty? Madness and Beauty?

Much love,
Jan Schrella

A h, nights are for dreaming, don't you think? Young people everywhere with the windows open . . . It would be so nice not to be working, not to have a job to do . . ."

"If you want, we can go out on the terrace. A little fresh air won't do us any harm."

"No. Let's continue. But try to be serious. I'm telling you this for your own good, for your artistic future. Everything you say is being recorded."

"Where were we?"

"No idea."

"Then let's go back to the night when Boris Lejeune is watching the enemy movements from the potato field."

"A nice boy . . . and a dreamer."

"Yes, he's in the habit of talking to himself."

"Like so many of us. I have a friend on the gossip pages who's always talking to herself. People think she's crazy; she'll probably lose her job. She spends the whole day muttering. Sometimes she rattles off the names of famous fashion designers. To herself or an invisible friend . . ."

"Boris Lejeune says, attention, attention . . ."

"Can he hear his own voice, or is he not even aware that his lips are moving, that random words are coming out?"

"Boris Lejeune here, attention, attention, failure of tanks R35, H35, H39, FCM36, D2, B1, FT17, S35, AMR, AMC . . . Where I'm from, it's normal to talk to yourself. . . . The Civil War is unstoppable. . . . It's like reciting from memory. . . . Special message for my lost friends: Vaché and Nizan can finally join ranks with Daudet and Maurras. . . . God doesn't exist. . . . The human race is scum. . . . Shit fuck cunt . . . Et cetera . . . Across the potato field, the lights blink like beings from another planet."

"I'm cold. This corner is freezing. What happens next?"

"Next, everything speeds up. The girl walks along the outskirts of Santa Bárbara. The caretaker goes for a ride on his bicycle. The machines at the academy work imperturbably, day and night, picking up curses and tantrums. The images begin to fall into place, each ready to be assigned its numbered spot on the map drawn with a firm hand and winged imagination by Dr. Huachofeo in his *Paradoxical History of Latin America*. Scene number one: A prisoner leaves a Paris jail, destined for a German concentration camp. In a station outbuilding, before he is put on the train, he's asked his name, for form's sake. I shit on your dead, the prisoner replies. In Spanish. What? asks the German soldier or the French gendarme. Boris Gutiérrez, says the prisoner.

Scene number two: A Spitfire plummets outside Southampton. The staff at the base watch from the ground. Why doesn't he jump? Who's flying that plane? They try to make radio contact, but no one replies. Collision is imminent; the plane is in a nosedive. The radio operator keeps trying: Jump, jump, jump, is there anyone in that plane? Suddenly a distant voice answers: Boris McManus here, I'm crashing. . . . Scene number three: A party of guerrilla soldiers retreat to an area near Užice. In the early-morning hours, they find a comrade wounded in both legs lying next to a dead youth. The wounded soldier explains that the youth brought him here. The guerrillas examine the body. There are multiple wounds to the chest and head. He can't possibly have brought you here, says the leader. He's been dead for at least twenty-four hours. I swear, last night he dragged me away from the front line and brought me here! I passed out a couple of times. I was in a lot of pain. We talked. He told me stories to distract me. He told me that he liked horses. And . . . The guerrillas have to acknowledge that the wounded man could never have made it this far on his own. In the dead youth's pocket, they find his identification papers: Boris Voilinovic, student at the Sarajevo School of Mechanical Arts and Flight. Employee of the Unknown University."

an's eyes widened in alarm, as if to ask what the hell was going on. Smiling and trying to keep my voice calm, I explained that it was some friends. That's obvious, he said as the others began to file into the room one by one, giving him no time to get dressed or gather up the scattered papers, newspaper clippings, science fiction books, maps, and dictionaries that were piled around his mattress like a kind of library dump. This is my friend Jan, I muttered. Only Angélica and Estrellita heard me. When the last person had come in, Jan jumped up, his skinny ass exposed and his balls dangling golden, and in two or three swift movements, his back to the group, he jammed his papers under the mattress and got back into bed; then he smoothed his hair and cast a cold eye over the recent arrivals. I don't think we'd ever had so many people in our room.

"Jan," I said, "this is Angélica; this is her sister, Lola; this is Colina; this is Antonio; this is the Señora Estrellita we've talked about . . ."

"Just Estrellita," said Estrellita.

"Pleased to meet you," said Jan.

"This is Héctor, this is César and . . . Laura."

"Well, well, well," said Jan.

I turned red.

"This is Jan, my friend and comrade."

"Hello." Smiles all around.

"Good evening," said Jan, his voice not the least bit friendly.

"What a lovely young man," said Estrellita. "And his darling balls are the color of gold."

Jan laughed.

"It's true," I said.

"That means that he's destined for greatness. Golden balls are the mark of a young man capable of . . . great deeds."

"They're not exactly golden," said Jan.

"Shut up. She thinks they look golden, and so do I. That's all that matters."

"And I do, too," said Angélica.

"What's the mark of greatness for women, Estrellita?" asked Lola.

"Is there any wine?"

"Where are the glasses?"

"That's more complicated, sweetheart." Estrellita sat on the floor by the window, without taking off her coat. "A smile, a laugh. Though Eunice said it was in the gaze . . . but I believe it's the laugh that's the mark."

"Wait a minute. Then nobody with brown skin, nobody

from the Bronze Race would be destined for greatness, not to mention black people."

"There are only five glasses and two chairs. We'll have to share glasses."

"What do you know about testicles? How many balls have you seen in your life?"

"Not a lot, true," admitted Colina. "Maybe fifteen."

"There are many marks of identity, Colinita," said Estrellita. "For black people, it's the wake they leave, memory and a sense of vertigo . . ."

"Estrellita is so talkative tonight."

"It must be from the climb up five flights of stairs."

"Sit on the floor."

"She's used to climbing stairs and staying up late."

"So this is the only room in the place?" asked César.

"That's right, it's small."

"What were you hiding under the mattress?"

"Nothing!"

"You and I will have to share this glass."

Angélica sat down next to Jan, on the edge of the mattress.

"Yes," said Jan.

"Is it true that you never go out?"

"Who told you that?"

"Your friend Remo and José Arco."

"They lied to you. I go out every day. I love to walk along Insurgentes. Up and down, up and down, like a soldier in the Wehrmacht."

"Like what?"

"A soldier in the Wehrmacht," said Jan. "Did you notice the color of this building?"

"No, it's dark out," said Angélica. She smiled. She looked much more attractive here than at La Habana or her house.

"It's greenish gray. Like the Nazi field uniform."

"How do you know?"

"I've seen it in books. Pictures of the uniform. Exactly the same color as the front of this building."

"That's creepy," said Angélica.

"You won a poetry prize, didn't you?"

"Yes. Who told you that? Remo or José Arco?"

"Nobody. I read it somewhere."

They looked at each other for an instant without smiling, like two piranhas swimming in a vacuum chamber. Then Jan said, "I'd like to read something you've written."

Meanwhile I was looking at Laura, who was sitting at the other end of the room next to Lola Torrente, talking in a low voice. Every so often, our eyes met and we smiled, though not at first but centuries later, when we were eating the sandwiches that José Arco had gone out to buy at some place only he knew about, and even then we might not have been smiling because we liked each other, at least not openly, but because the energy radiated by Jan and Angélica, sitting still as statues or a blushing bride and bridegroom, was growing little by little in the tight confines of that room, and the rest of us—whether by photosynthesis or because that's how we were back then or because in that place and on that night there was no other way to be, I swear I don't know—began to smile at each other, more and more like brides and bridegrooms, eating and drinking deliberately and relentlessly, waiting for someone to plug in the dawn at the window under which Estrellita was sleeping.

Sunk in a cup of oil and lost was the arrival of the Torrente sisters' parents, the breakup of the party half an hour later, my suggestion that we continue the fun—what was left of it—on the rooftop, the ride through nighttime Mexico City in taxis, *rancheras* on the radio, the precision of the Mexican dawn! and the faces, imagined or glimpsed through the windows of other cars, plunging into the tunnel with the determination of actors or commandos and coming out the other end ready for love, exquisitely made-up. The only thing that was real (I mean supremely real) was Laura's smile from across the room, her meteorite smile, fading half smile, barely there smile, friend smile, smoke smile, knife-in-an-arsenal smile, pensive smile, and smile—finally—meeting mine without pretense: smiles sought, smiles seeking each other.

Still, the patient reader mustn't imagine that this was some kind of mime show. God save me from a girl able to smile so many different ways in a matter of minutes. No. All the smiles fit into one smile. And the eye of the lover is like the eye of the fly, which means that other smiles might have been projected onto Laura's lips, her teeth.

But even so, did it matter? After all, wasn't Laura gradually turning into everyone and everything? Like the immaculate and ill-starred mother of legend, like the immaculate and ill-starred Aztec princess, like the immaculate and ill-starred wanderer of Tepeyac, like the immaculate and ill-starred Llorona, like the ghost of María Félix . . .

I leaped to my feet. I felt a little dizzy.

I announced that I was going down to the coffee shop two blocks away to buy sweet rolls. I asked for a volunteer to accompany me. Almost at the same instant, it occurred to me that José Arco might offer, and I was about to take back the request when Laura said, I'll go, I won't be long.

Who was she talking to when she said she wouldn't be long? César?

As I was counting the money that people gave me, I couldn't stop shaking and singing inside.

"This is a doll's house. I wish I had a place like this," she said as we went out.

The clouds, seen from the roof, seemed to suck up the electricity of the city; one even reached out a little arm that almost brushed the tallest buildings.

"It's going to rain," said Laura.

Her face, lit by the bulb hanging over the door to our room, seemed to turn transparent for an instant, silver for a fraction of a second, her brown eyes its only living, earthly feature.

"Do you know what name I'd give you?" I said as we were going down the stairs.

"Me?" she said, laughing as she passed Señor Ruvalcava's door.

"That's right."

"Why would you want to give me another name? Don't you like the one I have?" she asked in the lobby as I opened the door.

"I like your name a lot. It's just something that occurred to me up there, all of a sudden. But never mind. I'm erasing it."

"Now you have to tell me what it was."

"No, it's erased."

"What's the name?"

"Swear you won't get mad."

"That depends. Tell me what it is."

"Listen, really, don't ever get mad at me. I'd be a wreck." I laughed stupidly, but I meant it.

"What's the name? I can't promise."

"Aztec Princess."

Laura burst out laughing. It really was dumb, and I laughed, too. God, what an ass I am, I said. You really are, said Laura. We turned off Insurgentes. Just as I expected, the coffee shop was still open.

(A few days later, I described this conversation to José Arco. Funny, he said, there's a motorcycle called Aztec Princess. It's a brown motorcycle, a Benelli, big, not too banged up, and the name is painted on the tank in silver letters. If you want, we can go and see it. Why? I asked. It's a stolen bike, you could get it for cheap. No, I said, forget about it. I don't know how to ride, I'm not interested. The guy who has it is a poet, said José Arco. His name is Mofles. You'd like him. But I hardly have enough money for food, I said. I don't even have a driver's license, and anyway I don't like that shit. I hate those piece-of-crap bikes. Fine, fine, said José Arco.)

"Sometimes," I said to Laura, "it's open all night, other times it closes at six with no warning. It has no regular schedule."

"Nice place. Just a little run-down."

"It's called La Flor de Irapuato. I guess the owner doesn't care about appearances."

"Why not Flower of Peking or Flower of Shanghai?"

"Because the owner was born in Irapuato. Only his honorable grandparents were born in China. Canton, probably, but I could be wrong."

"Did he tell you so?"

"Emilio Wong, owner, cook, and sole waiter. If you want, we can have coffee before we go back. You can ask him why his schedule is so out of whack."

"Why is your schedule so strange? Remo told me about it; it's the first time I've been here."

"It's not really so strange," said Emilio Wong. "It's flexible and sometimes unexpected, but not strange."

"He makes great biscuits," I said.

"Remo told me that sometimes you don't close until dawn."

"Heh, it must be the nights I have insomnia."

"What I didn't tell you is that when Emilio has insomnia,

he writes poems. Please, don't ask him to read us one. He's thinking of selling his business in a few years and moving to Brazil."

"By van," said Emilio.

"Why don't you want him to read us a poem?"

"Can't you guess? He's a follower of the brothers Campos."

"Who are they?"

Laura's face shone in the dim sand-colored lights that hung over the counter. Across the counter, Emilio Wong furrowed his brow in sympathy. It seemed to me then that I had found the love of my life. I wanted to tell Laura, but she and Emilio were laughing. The coffee-shop owner said something about keeping a travel diary, a concrete or visual one, or maybe it was Laura who asked about it before turning to me and confessing that she would like that, too. Brazil? Traveling by van? Owning a coffee shop? I'd like to have a place like this, I said. Laura's face lit up and went dark. It wasn't the lights: sometimes her hair was blond, and sometimes it was brown, and sometimes she looked at me sort of very calmly, although in the mirror her eyes were like slow-motion arrows—sad, distant arrows—and I wondered why her pretty, dark eyes looked like that as family trees sprang to life and vanished over the counter: the Wongs of Canton, the Wongs of San Francisco and Los Angeles, the Wongs of Tijuana, and the Wongs who headed south across the border, not the usual thing for a Chinese couple settled in California, leaving behind a string of failed businesses before they arrived in Irapuato and died there. And Laura in the middle, nodding sympathetically, exclaiming in wonder, agreeing when Emilio said that his grandparents must have had good reason to leave San Francisco, that the mafia of cooks and laundrymen is merciless, and what could be more horrible than dying in a steamy kitchen or laundry, worse than Jack the Ripper's London fog. She expressed delight at the recipes for pig and fried snake and grilled strawberries, assuring him that he had a nice coffee shop, very original, and that she would be back another day for sure, begging him not to sell it, he should rent it to her when he was finally ready to leave for Brazil.

"The brothers Campos thing . . . it was a dumb joke. Sorry."

"That's okay," said Laura. "You're forgiven."

We finished our coffee.

Emilio had wrapped the sweet rolls in brown paper.

"Well, we're going."

"It makes me feel bad to leave Emilio here alone," I said.

"Why doesn't he come with us?"

"Oh, no, I'm used to it, don't be silly," said Emilio.

Once we were outside, Laura seemed different. All her enthusiasm had vanished. We walked back without saying a word. We were going up the stairs when she said, "I have to warn you, Remo, I'm a bad person."

She said it in a low voice, almost inaudible. In the darkness on the stairs, I got the sense that she was smiling.

"I don't believe it."

Laura stopped.

"It's true, I'm terrible, little things upset me, and I take it out on other people. Sometimes I think I'll end up murdering someone or that I'm going crazy."

"You're kidding," I said as I brought my face to hers and kissed her lips.

I had never wanted to kiss anyone as much as I wanted to kiss Laura.

"You see? I wanted you to kiss me, though when I tell César, I know it will hurt him."

"When will you tell him?"

"Not tonight, obviously."

"That's a relief."

Laura's eyes shone as they had in La Flor de Irapuato. I felt lost and happy there on the stairs. The stairs themselves, which had never had any special meaning, were transformed into something extraordinary, part snake and part precipice.

"I've never fallen in love before," I almost shouted.

"Are you in love with me?"

"I think so, but don't worry. It's the way I was brought up; I'm deeply and truly in love."

A sad smile appeared on Laura's face. For an instant, instead of flesh-and-blood people we were two cartoon characters. I said: "I feel like we're two cartoon characters pasted onto the real world. Or maybe the world isn't so real after all."

"Hansel and Gretel? Snow White and the Seven Dwarfs?" asked Laura.

"I don't know. I'm going to touch your breast to check."

"All right. Touch it."

I stroked her right breast, then the left, then I sighed and laughed a dumb laugh, hee-hee. "Yeah, this is the stepmother, and the other one is her mirror."

"You sound like Br'er Rabbit," said Laura as she kissed me.

The stairs seemed to writhe. Above us, though far enough away that we were still in the dark, a light shone. Laura asked me what I was looking at. I pointed out the brightness, which was swelling and growing nearer.

"It's like the stairs are tilting," I said.

It was true. The light was almost directly over our heads.

"Your lips are delicious," I said.

"Yours, too. Salty."

I licked our lips. Hers tasted like herbs and goat's milk (what kind of milk did Emilio Wong put in his coffee?), but I didn't tell her that.

"Are you really in love?"

"Of course."

"But why? Today I was feeling so bad. I went to see Lola because I was depressed; it was obvious, wasn't it?"

"When I saw you at the door, I fell in love with you. You looked serious."

"Poor César didn't want to come. I've been dragging him around all day. And only for his car, I think."

"Such a practical, honest girl," I said admiringly.

Laura smiled in satisfaction and kissed me once more. We clung together as if we would never see each other again.

"We could make love right here, and no one would know. This is such a strange building," she said.

"Jan says it's a totem of the Wehrmacht," I said. "I don't think I could."

"What do you mean, you don't think you could? You mean you couldn't fuck?"

"Yeah. I couldn't get it up. I couldn't get an erection. It's the way I am."

"You don't get erections?"

"No. I mean, I do, but it wouldn't work right now. This is a special moment for me, if that makes sense, and it's erotic, too, but there's no erection. Look, feel." I took her hand and put it to my crotch.

"You're right, it's not erect," said Laura with a barely audible laugh. "That's unusual for a guy. Maybe it's the stairs."

"The stairs have nothing to do with it."

Laura didn't move her hand from my penis.

"Maybe you're scared."

"The tiniest bit."

"You aren't a virgin, are you?"

I could barely hear her; her words came out amid muffled laughter, more luminous than the light spilling down from the landing.

"More or less. Anyway, it's a long story. But I swear I don't plan to die a virgin," I said.

"Oh."

She took her hand away, thoughtful for a second, and

then added, "I liked your Chinese friend. Tell me, seriously now, is he a poet, too?"

"Yes. My God, I hope it doesn't bother you that I can't get it up."

"It doesn't."

"Oh, no, I think it does."

"No, silly, it really doesn't. I don't like it when you say that you're in love with me. That's all. Let's go up. They must think something happened to us."

From the roof, the sky looked charged with the same intensity as when we had left. Fat black clouds were crowded aside or shot through by filaments of purple clouds. From far off came the sound of the rain, though in this part of the city not a drop was falling. Before we went into the room, Laura turned and kissed me on the cheek. As she was moving away, I grabbed her by the shoulders. Through the door, we could hear our friends' voices. "I'd like to keep talking to you," I said. It definitely didn't come out right. We smiled at each other, utterly remote. I hope it pours, I thought.

"Aztec Princess, huh. Funny," she murmured. "What made you think of that?"

"I told you. I don't know."

We went in. Jan was talking at the top of his lungs. He waved to us, raising a glass. He was completely drunk. I sat down on the floor, and soon there was a glass in my hand, too.

D o you really think this is normal? I mean, are these artsy parties normal for Mexico? I can't help feeling that there's something unhealthy about all this. Something sad and dark."

"It's true. People drink. They aren't careful. The celebrating gets out of hand. That's the way it always is."

"Good thing I have someone to talk to. If I were alone, I would've left by now."

"That might've been a little difficult. The winner isn't allowed to just walk out of a party thrown in his honor . . ."

"I was afraid of that."

"My poor friend, don't look so gloomy. Let's talk more about your work. Why are your stories always set in Europe? Don't you know that true universality lies in the particular, the local?"

"Please don't talk that way. You sound like the long-lost sister of the Taviani brothers. The truth is, and I'm not saying this to get off the hook, no part of my humble first work is set in Europe. There are references to books read in child-hood, part nostalgia, part desperation. Magazines I can barely remember: *U-2, Commando, Spitfire,* maybe, though they probably had other names. . . . It can also be seen as an interpretation of the teachings of Huachofeo: extrapolation leads us to open doors that were once bricked up. . . . A very southern turn of phrase, straight out of Concepción. . . . But ask me questions. I don't want to bore you."

"You aren't boring me. I've got the shivers. Did you say we're in a clearing in the woods?"

"Let's go out on the terrace, and you can see for yourself. Or let's open this window. I don't think anyone will notice."

"No, don't do it. Soon enough the two of us will stroll out arm in arm for a breath of fresh air. Right now I think it would make me sick. Talk to me about something, anything. About new Mexican poetry."

"For God's sake. I insist: you aren't well. Let's get out of this hole or at least have a cup of coffee. It smells like semen and vaginal juices in here!"

"You're right. Old people's semen and vaginal juices."

"Old intellectuals', I might add."

"Talk to me about your work; if we keep this up, I'll probably lose my job."

"You'd get plenty of offers. You're a very nice reporter."

"Thank you."

"And incredibly hardworking."

"Thank you. If you don't mind, let's stay on the subject."

Dear Ursula K. Le Guin:

I wrote you a letter, but luckily I didn't send it: it was a pretentious letter, full of questions that you've already answered one way or another in your beautiful books. I'm seventeen, and I was born in Chile, but now I live on a rooftop in Mexico City, with views of incredible sunrises. There are a number of rooms on the roof, but only five are inhabited. I live in one of them with a friend who claims to be from Chile. In another room—let's call it the second room, though I'm not following any particular order— lives a domestic, also known as a servant or maid or housekeeper or the help, with her four small children. In the third lives a housekeeper for one of the apartments, the one belonging to Mr. Ruvalcava. In the fourth lives an old man whose last name is Mirror; he doesn't go out much, but neither do I, so never mind. In the fifth lives a woman, about forty-five, perfectly groomed and elegant, who disappears early each morning and doesn't come

back until past ten at night. Along what you might call
the roof's central corridor, bordered by flowerpots that
give it a cheerful tropical air, there are three shower
stalls and two toilets, all tiny, though comfortable, with
sturdy wooden doors. The showers are cold-water, except
for one, which has a boiler that runs on sawdust—it
belongs to the mother of four and is private and has a
lock—but in general that isn't a problem, except on rare
occasions when the days are so cold that good hygiene is
impossible. We wash our faces and hands at the laundry
sinks in a side corridor. It's an eight-story building, and
my room overlooks the avenue, which I'm able to admire
from our only window (it's a big window at least), never
failing to marvel at its length and brightness. My
mattress, like my friend's, sits on the floor, a curious
floor of mustard-yellow and brown bricks, and it's from
here that I write letters and drafts of something that one
of these days might become a science fiction novel. It's
not easy, I admit. I try to learn, study, observe, but I
always come to the same conclusion: it's not easy, and I'm
in Latin America; it's not easy, and I'm Latin American;
it's not easy, and to add insult to injury, I was born in
Chile, though Hugo Correa (does the name ring a bell?)
might beg to differ. Regarding the letters, they're all
addressed to science fiction writers in the United States,
writers who might reasonably be supposed to be alive
and whom I like: James Tiptree Jr., Theodore Sturgeon,
Ray Bradbury, R. A. Lafferty, Fritz Leiber, Alfred Bester.

(If only I could communicate with the dead, I would write to Philip K. Dick.) I don't think many of my missives will reach their destination, but it's my *duty* to hope with all my might and keep sending them. I get the addresses from sci-fi fanzines, and lots of the letters are even sent directly to fanzines in different parts of the United States in hopes that their editors will forward the messages to their (presumably) favorite writers. Other letters are addressed to publishing houses, some to literary agencies (especially the famous Spiderman brothers), and a few to the writers' home addresses. I tell you all this so that you don't think it's a simple task. Actually it is, but I could convince anyone otherwise. Really, I guess I can state objectively that all I do is write letter after letter to people I'll probably never meet. It's funny: you could say that it's like using the radio before the ansible was invented, ha-ha. Years and years of waiting to receive an enigmatic reply. But I suppose that's not the case, and even if it was, there's no point making a big deal about it. Oh, Ursula, it's actually a relief to send out messages and have all the time in the world, to say I tried to convince them but that's as far as it went, to have strange but peaceful dreams. . . . Though the dreams are becoming less peaceful. I read that one out of every ten Americans has dreamed of nuclear missiles shooting across a starry sky. It might have been more; it may be that many would rather forget what they dreamed. In Latin America, I'm afraid, sleep is linked to other demons. One in twenty has dreamed of Abraham and Isaac on the mount. One in ten has dreamed of the flight to Egypt. One in five has dreamed of *Quo Vadis* and Victor Mature. But there's another nightmare, the main one, forgotten by poll responders at the first light of dawn and the first howl of the alarm clock. All, without exception, report that at least once in their lives they've suffered through the Key Nightmare, but no one remembers it. Shadowy figures, unintelligible words, and the dreamer's sense, upon awakening, that he possesses a third lung or maybe has lost one over the course of the night—that's all we know. And I'll leave it at that. It's eight in the morning, we threw a nice party in our room, but now I'm tired. Everything is a mess! I'm alone. I'll go brush my teeth at one of the sinks, and then I'll hang a black cloth over the window and go to sleep. . . . Why do I write letters, you ask? . . . Maybe just to be a pain in the ass, or maybe not. . . . Maybe I've lost my mind from reading so many science fiction novels. . . . Maybe the letters are my NAFAL ships. . . . In any case, and most important, please accept my eternal gratitude.

Warmly,
Jan Schrella

I tried to drink. I tried to laugh at words caught in passing that weren't meant to be funny. I woke Estrellita up from peaceful sleep, from a place far away from the rooftop and everyone's prophecies of triumph, with a cup of tea that the old woman drank with a smile before falling back to sleep. (I felt terrible.) I tried to seem lost in thought, oblivious, invisible, leafing through a book of literary criticism amid the din; I really just wanted everyone to leave so I could turn out the lights and drop onto my mattress. At a certain point, people began to vanish. Jan got dressed and went out into the corridor with José Arco and the Torrente sisters. Then Pepe Colina vanished. I wasn't alarmed until Laura and César left, the latter apparently drunker than I was. I felt depressed. It seemed best not to move, to sit still and wait. My depression morphed smoothly into despair. Héctor, Estrellita, and I were the only ones left in the room, which was suddenly huge. Then someone said that Angélica had felt sick and they'd taken her out for a walk on the roof. Like in a horror movie, the walkers hadn't kept together for long: Jan and Angélica went into one of the toilet stalls, and José Arco and Lola smoked a cigarette under the clotheslines, where they were joined by Pepe Colina. I can't remember how long it was before the door opened again and everybody reappeared one by one. Before the last person came in, I jumped up, unable to bear the possibility that Laura wasn't among them. But there she was, and when our eyes met, I realized that whatever there was between us wouldn't end that night. The night itself did end at some point, though it seemed interminable.

I should ask someone or check in an almanac, because sometimes I'm sure it was the longest night of the year. What's more, sometimes I could swear that it didn't end the way nights always end, swallowed up all of a sudden or chewed over by a slow dawn. The night I'm talking about— cat night, nine-lives night in twenty-league boots—vanished or ebbed in odd moments, and as it was going, part of it (and therefore all of it) was coming or lingering, like in some game of mirrors. The nicest kind of hydra: 6:30 A.M. transforming itself unexpectedly into 3:15 for five minutes, a phenomenon that might strike some as annoying but that for others was a blessing, a genuine reprieve and a rewinding.

2

I dreamed of the Russian cosmonaut. . . . Now I know who it is . . ."

"Oh, really?"

"Belyaev . . . Alexander Belyaev . . ."

"What cosmonaut? What are you talking about?"

"A figure approaches a kind of cell or waiting room, where I am. . . . A soft, grayish cubicle . . . Between the two of us, there's some kind of mesh, so it isn't hard for me to see what's outside, to see where Belyaev is coming from."

"My whole body aches. . . . What time is it?"

"Six, six P.M."

"Ugh, disgusting. . . . What are you doing in bed?"

"I went to bed an hour ago, in solidarity, so that we would be on the same schedule . . ."

"Sure, ha-ha . . . When I got back, you were sleeping like a log."

"I was asleep, but I woke up. I made lunch, showered, did some work, and went back to sleep. . . . Why don't you take the black cloth off the window? . . . Now, listen: behind the mesh, there was an airport . . ."

"Of course."

"Beyond the airport, at the edge of a plain, there was a clear view of two mountains silhouetted against the sky. . . . At the beginning of the dream, we were both looking in that direction, but then he came over to me and introduced himself politely, with a smile. . . . It was Alexander Belyaev. . . . Do you know who he is?"

"No idea, Jan."

"A science-fiction writer."

"I thought so. . . . Have you ever read Tolstoy, Bulgakov?"

"Not much . . ."

"I'm not surprised. . . . You should read other Russian writers, other writers in general. You can't spend your life reading stories about spaceships and extraterrestrials."

"Don't bait me. And listen, this is fun: The airport actually looked like a tennis court, and the mountains were like two pyramids made out of papier-mâché. . . . But if you looked carefully, there was something about it, an unreal glow over everything, and Belyaev knew it and wanted me to see it. . . . Something in his eyes, shadowed by the visor of the space helmet, testified vividly to the incorporeal presence of other people . . . *la troupé*, invisible . . . an energy field . . ."

"What . . . ?"

"I don't understand a thing, I said to him. My knowledge

of physics is nil, and in high school all I did was write poems. I wanted to cry with impotence. . . . In dreams, when the tears come, everything gradually goes dark or fades to pure white. . . . Then he spoke for the first time; I could see his lips move, deliberately, though his voice blared from somewhere else, as if there were hidden speakers in the little room: I'm Alexander Belyaev, he said, Soviet citizen and professor at the Unknown University . . ."

"What is the Unknown University?"

"A university that no one has ever heard of, obviously. Alfred Bester mentions it in a story. But Belyaev—as I'm sure you don't know—was born in Smolensk in 1884 and starved to death in January of '42, in Leningrad."

"Poor fucker . . ."

"Then Belyaev turned away from me and vanished. Across the plain came a very strong wind and then some black storm clouds; colors, however, had never been so bright. I thought that this was what death must be like. I felt trapped inside a postcard, while at the same time I was paradoxically watching the landscape slip away. Until the net came loose on the tennis court. It was very strange. It suddenly came unhooked and floated down like a feather. I was sure that no one would ever play there again. And I woke up. You were talking in your sleep."

"Was I?"

"Yes. How did it go with Laura?"

"Fine. How was it here?"

"A scene. I don't think I'll ask them up again. They're too belligerent when they drink: César got into a fistfight with José Arco. Luckily, he didn't pick me as scapegoat."

"Scapegoats have nothing to do with it, Jan. Anyway, I can stand up for myself. . . . Who won?"

"Our friend, of course, but with a little help."

"Don't tell me you ganged up on poor César."

"It would be more correct to say that we held him down. José Arco was the only one who hit him."

"What a bunch of cowards. Really, I can't believe it."

"Heh-heh-heh."

"I'm not surprised that you dreamed of Belyaev, then. It must be your guilty conscience gnawing at you."

"Call it self-defense. Your rival is one tough nut. Anyway, if it were me, I would tread carefully. Before he left, he swore that he would make you pay—multiple times over, naturally—for every punch that José Arco got in. Though there weren't many, to be honest."

"What will Laura think?"

"He said something about Laura, too, but I'll keep it to myself. I don't know what you were thinking, leaving with Laura just then. César was desperate. He spent a long time looking for the two of you on the roof. Maybe he thought you were hiding in one of the toilets, which is pretty standard practice, I can tell you from experience. When he came back to the room without you, he blew up. By the way, where did you go?"

"We walked to Chapultepec, talking all the way. Then we had breakfast together, and I took her to the Metro."

"See? César imagined you were at a sleazy hotel."

"What an ass."

"Fortunately, our José Arco turns out to be good with his fists, though I can tell you he's no stylist; he's more of a slugger. But listen to this: during the fight, your rival did his best to break as many objects as possible in this, your humble abode. Whereas José Arco worried more about the glasses, books, and fingers scattered around on the floor than his own face."

"One of these days, his gallantry will get him killed."

"Knock on wood. . . . In any case, the thing ended well. Between us, Angélica and I kicked out the thwarted suitor. Not a drop of blood was spilled. Estrellita's sleep was only disturbed when it was time to leave. I turned down Colina and Mendoza's invitation to come with the group in search of a restaurant that was open for breakfast. Once I had said I wasn't coming, Mendoza seized the opportunity to make an exit with his arm around Angélica's waist. A well-intentioned gesture if you consider that it must have been seven in the morning or something. An angelic gesture, even, but that's really not my main concern right now. Lola and Héctor left before the fight. José Arco stayed for a while, and the two of us cleaned up the mess a little. Mostly what we did was fall around laughing at your César and everybody else. Finally he left, too, and I lay down on the mattress. But I didn't sleep: I wrote a letter to Ursula Le Guin. Could you mail it for me today?"

"Of course. What do you say in the letter?"

"I talk about dreams and the Revolution."

"Nothing about the Unknown University?"

"No . . ."

"Why don't you ask her if she knows where to find it?"

The days (or hours) that followed were exceedingly sweet, in many people's opinions. Up until then, I had been an onlooker in Mexico City, a fairly pretentious recent arrival and a clumsy twenty-one-year-old poet. The city, I mean, took no notice of me, and my dreams never escaped the confines of pedantry and deadly artifice. (Oh, if nothing had happened or at least if Jan and José Arco had kept their mouths shut, instead of being where I am now, I'd be in the Paradise of Latin American Men of Letters—in other words, teaching at an American university or at worst correcting galleys at a second-rate publishing house, peaceful haven, infinite promise.) Still, the days were sweet. Very sweet. Jan and José Arco immersed themselves in calculations and conjectures that we could never have imagined. My status as onlooker persisted, but with a new twist: the seeing eye was able to transmute itself into the streets and objects that it observed, which is what someone (Chateaubriand? the Prophet of the Crossroads?) once called a dry orgasm. At the call of the Aztec Princess, projects, poems, the cult of pocketbook and prudence were abandoned—everything, except for Mexico City (which adopted me overnight) and Lewis Carroll. Our everyday existence was suddenly upset: romantic rendezvous blossomed on one side and the pleasures of the labyrinth and the tangled web on the other. José Arco landed a meeting with Dr. Ireneo Carvajal. Pepe Colina, when we told him about the existence of the *Conasupo Weekly,* gave us the address of someone by the name of Leonardo Díaz, a poet devoted body and soul to literary paradoxes. Jan's letters to the United States multiplied. In my dreams, Laura actually said onward! set out in search of the Hurricane, against a backdrop of alpine scenery, her hair bright and electrified. In real life, Laura said I love you, we're going to be very happy. And very good! I added. We have to be good and generous, Laura! We have to be compassionate and selfless! Laura laughed, but I was serious. One afternoon, I'll never forget it, as we were going up the escalator in the Metro, I did a tap dance. That was all. I had never tried anything like it, and it came out perfect. Laura said, you do that so well. You're the spitting image of Fred Astaire. I was surprised. I shrugged, and my eyes filled with tears.

"Why are you sad?"

"I don't know, but I feel like I've been torn apart," I said.

"All because you did a tap dance? Poor thing, come here and let me give you a hug."

"Let's stay like this with our arms around each other, okay?"

"But then we'll be in the way of people getting off."

"Well, then we'll get off, too, but slowly."

And the echo: we have to be good and generous, Laura! We have to be compassionate and selfless, because otherwise terror will turn its gaze on us! And Laura laughed, of course, and I did, too, but my laughter wasn't as confident.

As for Jan, his letters multiplied, as I've said. In fact, he spent most of the day writing letters and reading science fiction books that José Arco and I brought him by the cart-load. The books were almost all stolen, which was easy enough with the assistance of José Arco, who was untiring in such pursuits. It was no simple thing to deliver the list of titles and authors that Jan required. Many of them hadn't been translated into Spanish yet and needed to be lifted from specialty English bookstores, which were few and far between in Mexico City and, what's worse, equipped with private security more suited to the library at Alcatraz. Still, after some near misses, Jan had all the books he wanted at his disposal. These books, underlined, scribbled on, and under-lined again, piled up so chaotically in every corner of the room that it could be hard to get around; going out to pee in the middle of the night when you weren't quite awake, without turning on the light, could be dangerous: pests like E. E. Smith—the little rat—or Olaf Stapledon, or the near-complete works of Philip K. Dick posing as a boulder could trip you when you least expected it. It wasn't unusual to wake up from a nightmare with a book by Brian Aldiss or the brothers Strugatsky wrapping itself around your feet, and it was useless, of course, to conjecture how the book in question had ended up in that precise spot, though I have to admit that we didn't make our beds too frequently. (I don't think I can be accused of being dramatic when I say that I was once woken by my own cries: not only was I kicking at a book, but I had gripped its pages between my toes like a monkey, and to make matters worse, one of my feet had fallen asleep and my toes, against all logic, curled around the pages and refused to let go.) Until finally Jan decided to tidy up that galactic trash heap. One early afternoon, all the books turned up stacked against the wall, but in such a way that instead of a pile of books it looked like a bench in the town square. The only things missing were the trees and pigeons, but the feel of a bench in a plaza, the aura of it, radiated from the pile of stolen volumes. Almost immediately I realized that this was precisely the intent.

"How did you do it?" I exclaimed in surprise.

"With patience." Jan looked strange, overexcited, his skin almost transparent.

"It reminds me of . . . the benches in the Plaza de Armas in Los Ángeles."

"Moral of the story: never underestimate the paperback."

The next day the bench disappeared, or rather it metamorphosed into a modernist table about fifteen inches tall, a solid mass of books with a couple of tunnels that opened on two of its five sides, then met at the center and came out together on the far side, the side full of edges. To drive home the joke, Jan had set a glass of water with a flower in it in the middle of the table, on the cover of a book by John Varley.

"Señora Estela's daughter gave me the carnation."

"Very pretty, Jan, very pretty . . ."

"Hmm, yeah, not bad . . . We can even eat on it, if you want; it's sturdy, but we'll have to find something to use as a tablecloth, okay? I don't want you getting food on any of the books."

"No, man, you've got to be kidding. Let's eat at the real table."

"Why? Look, touch it, it's strong, well made."

We had lunch there, on the books covered by a light blanket, and dinner, too—José Arco was with us, and at first he didn't believe it, so we had to lift the blanket so he could see that the table was made of books. That night, before he went to sleep, Jan actually suggested that I could write at the table if I wanted to. I flatly refused.

After a while, I asked him, "Did you sit?"

Jan's eyes were closed, and he looked asleep, but he answered in a clear voice.

"No."

"Did you think the bench wouldn't hold you?"

"No, it wasn't that."

"Why didn't you sit, then? Or why didn't you ask me to sit?"

"I was . . . afraid. . . . No, not afraid . . . It made me feel sad. Sad deep inside. Shit, that sounds like a *corrido*."

"No, like a bolero . . . Heh-heh-heh . . . Good night, Jan, sweet dreams."

"Good night, Remo, write good things."

Then I was the one who was scared. It wasn't sadness or uneasiness. It was fear. There, with a cigarette hanging from my lips, the room lit only by the glow of the lamp, my friend about to start snoring and fall asleep for real (God willing), and the city spinning outside.

But sunrise came, and the fear went away. It was a sunrise that said hello, hello, little cowards, hello, hello. Do you know who I am? as it pushed on the windowpane and pressed our shadows against the wall. Of course, I said. Five minutes later, half asleep and pulling the sheet over his head, Jan said: of course, you're the incredible sunrise that promised to show up every three days. Exactly, exactly, said the sunrise, and we yawned, made tea—kind of a pain in the ass, this sunrise, don't you think?—we smoked, we told each other our dreams. Hello, hello, yippee! I'm the Mexican sunrise that always beats death.

"Of course," Jan said mockingly.

"Sure, why not," I murmured.

The earthly abode of Dr. Ireneo Carvajal was on the fourth floor of a 1950s apartment building in a working-class neighborhood with lots of kids—there was a day care on the fifth floor, to judge by the noise—and a notable lack of the silence and mystery in which José Arco and I had wreathed the director of the *Poetry Bulletin of Mexico City*. The doctor received us in a tobacco-colored robe that fell to his shins and seemed excessive considering the heat of the day; he was a thin man of indeterminate age, between forty and sixty, his angular face scored by precise and symmetrical wrinkles. His bearing was that of someone sad and well bred. In contrast to the living-room furnishings, which were tidy and petit bourgeois, the collar of his shirt showed signs of neglect or poverty. He avoided our eyes, listening to us in silence with his gaze fixed on the floor or the foot of an armchair, and as José Arco explained why we had come, he began to bite his lips more and more furiously, as if our presence was suddenly a strain. When at last he spoke, I thought it would be to show us out. I was wrong.

"Boys," he said, "I fail to understand why you're so interested in a perfectly ordinary phenomenon."

"Don't you think it's odd, to say the least, that there are more than six hundred literary magazines in Mexico City?"

Dr. Carvajal smiled benevolently.

"Let's not exaggerate. My esteemed friend Ubaldo, always so seismic, has gotten himself all worked up about nothing. Six hundred literary magazines? It depends on what you call a magazine and how you define literature. More than a quarter of these magazines are really a few sheets of paper, photocopied and stapled in runs of twenty at best, sometimes fewer. Literature? According to me, yes; according to Octavio Paz, for example, no; scribbles, shadows, diary entries, sentences as mysterious as a telephone directory; from a professor's perspective, they're a distant jet trail, the faint echo of a nameless failure; from a policeman's perspective, they're not even anything subversive. No matter who you ask, they're essentially texts outside the realm of literary history. Of course, heh-heh, I'm not talking about government publications."

"It still seems incredible to me—excuse me, I mean disturbing. Don Ubaldo told us that he didn't think there were more than two hundred magazines published in Mexico City last year."

"In *My Enchanted Garden*," I added, "you say that by the

end of the year there may be more than a thousand, enough to make *The Guinness Book of World Records.*"

"Maybe," said Dr. Carvajal, shrugging his shoulders. "But even so, I fail to see why it matters to you. . . . Do you want to prove that a record was set? Compile an anthology of rare texts? Let me disabuse you of that notion: There are no rare texts. Wretched ones, to be sure, and luminous ones, but none of them rare."

"They interest us as a symptom."

"A symptom of what?"

José Arco didn't answer. I guessed that my friend was thinking about the Hurricane. Dr. Carvajal got up with an enigmatic smile and left the room. He came back with a few of the magazines.

"Photocopied sheets, mimeographed sheets, even hand-written sheets, the output of poetry workshops for self-proclaimed orphans, modern-music fanzines, song lyrics, a drama in verse on the death of Cuauhtémoc, all with the occasional spelling mistake, all humbly situated in the very center of the world . . . *Ay,* Mexico . . ."

The magazines, scattered on the table that separated our armchairs from our host's wooden chair, seemed as skeletal as the prisoners of Nazi concentration camps. Like those emaciated figures, or like the photographs we see of them, I mean, they were black and white and had big, hollow eyes. I thought: they have eyes, they're looking at us. Then, feigning a calm that I suddenly didn't feel, I said, "They do look pretty pathetic," and right away I felt like an idiot.

"A symptom of the Revolution." José Arco's voice, unlike mine, sounded firm and confident, though I could tell that he was bluffing.

"Such arrogance!" exclaimed the doctor. "Though the producers of these sheets would be thrilled to hear you say so. To me, the magazines are the symptom of a certain kind of unhappiness. Let me tell you another story that will surely be a lesson to us; it comes from the book *Ten Years in Africa* by the Chiapas priest Sabino Gutiérrez. The events narrated by Father Gutiérrez take place in a village near Kindu, in what was then the Belgian Congo. This was at some point in the 1920s, though Father Gutiérrez was in the village only twice, the first time to visit his friend Pierre Leclerc, a French missionary, and the second time to lay flowers on Leclerc's grave. Both visits were brief. In between, Gutiérrez traveled across southeast Congo to Lake Mweru, reaping no great evangelical rewards but finding delight as an incorrigible tourist, finally settling in Angola for eight months at least. This is when the events that I'm about to describe took place, and I believe that they are in some way related to what I fear you glimpse behind the small-magazine phenomenon, though they have little to do with the phenomenon itself. Before I continue, I must warn you that after years spent in Africa, mostly on trips and expeditions that for some reason are never fully explained, Father Gutiérrez wasn't easily surprised. And yet something about this village near Kindu awakened his curiosity: the natives displayed unusual manual dexterity, a talent for woodworking that he had never seen before. Or possibly it wasn't their skill that impressed him but their enthusiasm, the atmosphere. In a moving passage, he recalls his one stroll through the village with Leclerc, whom he had met in Rome and to whom he seems bound by true and deep friendship, though they have little in common. (Sabino Gutiérrez was worldly, learned, brilliant, the kind of man who would spend his time in Katanga revising his own translation of Pindar; Leclerc is described as kind-hearted, cheerful, a stranger to pomp and vanity.) As they walk, Gutiérrez peers into the huts and marvels at the wooden objects created by the collective exercise of the art of carpentry. Leclerc, peppered with questions by Gutiérrez, doesn't share his friend's astonishment: it was he who introduced many of the tools that the natives are using; he believes that what they're doing is good and healthy; he can't see what's so strange about it. Gutiérrez lets it go, but that night, the only night he spends in the town, he dreams of chairs, stools, cupboards, dressers, tables of all sizes (mostly small), benches, doghouses or dollhouses, and an infinite number of objects that can be separated into three categories: furniture in the strict sense; toys or imitations of European progress, like trains, cars, guns, et cetera; and unidentifiable or artistic objects, like irons with holes in them, toothed disks, enormous cylinders. The next day, before he leaves, Leclerc presents him with one of the wooden objects that he finds so discomfiting: a crucifix, three inches tall, carved from a soft, almost juicy wood, black with yellow streaks. Our traveler is delighted to accept it; it is certainly an excellent piece. The visit ends with effusive displays of affection on both sides and promises to meet up again before too long. Months later, once he's settled in Luanda, Sabino Gutiérrez receives a letter from his friend, who returns to the topic of woodworking in a lengthy postscript. It has become even more widespread now, says Leclerc, to the point that it occupies the whole town, with few exceptions. The villagers work their fields in a daze; the shepherds have lost interest in their flocks. Leclerc and the two nuns who work as nurses are beginning to worry. But the matter hardly merits grave concern; in fact, the Frenchman treats it as a joke. He even makes inquiries—ultimately fruitless—about selling the pieces in Léopoldville. After this, every time that Sabino Gutiérrez writes to his friend, he asks about the village woodworkers. The situation remains stable for six months. Then a new letter from Leclerc sounds the alarm. Woodworking fever has taken over the village and seems contagious: in some neighboring villages, men, women, and children are sawing with the only communal saw, hammering with the two communal hammers, sanding, assembling, gluing. The villagers make up for the lack of tools with imagination and indigenous craft. The finished objects pile up in huts and yards, overflowing the frenzied village. Leclerc speaks to the elders. The only reply he gets is the witch doctors' diagnosis: a virus of sadness and exaltation has seized the town. Despite himself, he is surprised to recognize a little sadness and exaltation in his own soul, like a tiny, twisted reflection of the emotions that have taken root in his village.

The next and final letter is brief; according to Sabino, it is written with the simplicity of a de Vigny and the desperation and religiosity of a Verlaine. (Ha-ha, as you can see, his critical methods aren't far removed from those of our contemporary reviewers.) One imagines that all this mattered not a whit to Leclerc by now. The narrow streets of the village are littered with wooden tools that no one has used or will use. The woodworkers gather in secret with delegations of woodworkers from elsewhere. Almost no one attends Mass. As a precaution, the priest has ordered the nuns to retreat to Kindu. He spends the tense, idle days whittling a crucifix—at this point, he asks Gutiérrez to throw away the crucifix that he gave him on his previous visit 'because compulsion perverts the figure of Christ' and promises that he will replace it with the 'carving that I'm working on now' or an 'Andalusian Christ worked in silver.' He laments the situation in the village. He wonders about the future of the children. He mourns his lost efforts. But he doesn't specify what he fears or where the threat lies. He does speak of the dead: white colonists killed, a strike attempt at a tin mine, but nothing else. You could say that all he cares about is his village and that nothing that happens outside its boundaries is real to him. On some level, he feels responsible; let us not forget that he was the woodworker-in-chief, in a sense. Now he can't even muster horror at the sight of the strange wooden tub that a group of teenagers has left in his vegetable patch. The end comes quickly. The nuns flee, presumably carrying the letter with them. Leclerc is left alone. Months later Gutiérrez learns of his death. Once the shock subsides, and after attempting in vain to make inquiries from Luanda, our priest pulls every string he can in order to return to the Congo, to the place where his friend was laid to rest. At last he succeeds. The problem now is the Belgian authorities who are reluctant to consent to the visit. The events at Village X are considered classified. Upon persisting, Gutiérrez discovers that Leclerc's death wasn't accidental. His friend was killed during a native uprising. Beyond that the official explanation is vague: perhaps there was a battle between two neighboring tribes, or maybe the witch doctors incited the slaughter. Based in Kindu, Gutiérrez leads an absolutely unorthodox life. Finally he obtains authorization to visit the village with a colonial official and a doctor. When they arrive, there is something ominous about the few huts left standing, the new dispensary, the living souls glimpsed through dark doorways, and the very air they breathe. The cemetery, exquisitely laid out, boasts an enormous number of new crosses. When Gutiérrez asks, he is informed that the nuns who worked here have returned to Europe. Of course everyone is reluctant to recall the woodworking that once went on in the village; there is no trace of the former craftspeople. Exasperated, our priest decides to visit his friend's grave on his own. Then he realizes that the crucifix that Leclerc asked him to get rid of is in his pocket. He takes it out and gives it one last look. The Jesus figure is strange, strong, serene; it even seems to smile when looked at from a certain angle. He hurls it into the underbrush. Instantly he realizes that he isn't alone; he first hears and then sees an old man creep out from behind a tree and feel around in the spot where the crucifix fell. Gutiérrez, frozen in fear, doesn't move. After searching for a moment, the old man gets up, and, without coming toward him—in fact, keeping his distance—he speaks. His name is Matala Mukadi, and he is going to tell Gutiérrez the truth. Leclerc was killed by the white men. Three hundred natives suffered the same fate, and bullets from the white men's guns surely rest in the bones of those who weren't burned to death. But why? asks Gutiérrez. Because of the revolt. The whole village rebelled. The miners rebelled. Everything happened all at once, like a miracle. And the whites crushed the rebellion thoroughly and completely: Women, children, and old people died. Those who sought refuge with the French priest were killed in the mission house itself, then half of the village was burned to the ground and the area was cordoned off. The whites had firearms; the natives had only wooden rifles, wooden pistols. Why did they kill Leclerc? asks Gutiérrez, and he expects that the black man will say that it was because he took up the cause of the woodworkers, but the old man is unequivocal: it was by chance. The slaughter was quick, of course. The black man holds up the little wooden figure. Magic? asks Gutiérrez before the other turns and leaves. No, says the black man: the clothes it wears, village clothes. Our priest understands that when he says 'village,' he means rage or sleep. They part without another word. From the moment that Gutiérrez gives more credence to the black man's account than to the white man's, there's little to be done. Two years later, he leaves Africa—and then Europe—forever. He returns to Chiapas, where he devotes himself to writing his memoirs and religious essays until the day he dies. His final years, if his editor (another priest) is to be believed, are placid and anonymous. And that's all . . ."

Dr. Carvajal was silent; his face, lit by the last rays of sun filtering in through the blinds, resembled a skull haphazardly covered by a film of skin. And yet there was something strong and healthy about his head.

"What I'm trying to tell you," he said at last, "is that six hundred little magazines give or take make no difference . . ."

"Whatever happens happens, you mean?" José Arco interrupted him.

"Precisely, young man, and the only thing an intellectual can do is watch things blow up, from a safe distance, of course."

"In my opinion," I said, leafing through the four pages of a publication ambiguously titled *Paradise Lost and Paradise Regained*, "the creators of these magazines are intellectuals, too."

"Yes," said José Arco, "motorcycle thieves."

Dr. Carvajal smiled in satisfaction; deep down he was a cinema-club neorealist.

"Victims," he said, and though he was smiling, his voice was terrible. "Oblivious players in a drama that in all likelihood I'll never witness. Or maybe not even that: a meaningless accident of fate. In the United States, they're getting into video, I have it on good authority. In London, teenagers play for a few months at being pop stars. And nothing comes of it, of course. Here, as you might expect, we seek out the cheapest and most pathetic drug or hobby: poetry, poetry magazines; that's just the way it is. There's no getting around the fact that this is the land of Cantinflas and Agustín Lara."

I was about to say that I thought he was wrong: back then I believed—and even now I may still believe—that Latin America's greatest literary successes came in verse form. To bad-mouth Vallejo, to lack an in-depth knowledge of the work of Gabriela Mistral, to confuse Huidobro with Reverdy: these were things that made me sick, and then angry. The poetry of our poor countries was a motive—maybe the main motive—of pride for the young Turk who took possession of my body once a week. But I didn't say any of this. Instead I remembered something that I'd read in Jan's collection of papers, and I connected it immediately to the subject of our conversation.

"I don't think that video is the Americans' drug, though actually I don't know whether you're talking about video games or making movies. But I can tell you that a new hobby is gaining ground: war-gaming. The range is pretty broad, though basically there are two main approaches: board games, played on a hexagonal grid with cardboard markers called counters, and weekend war games, like the ones we played when we were kids, except that the gringos who play them now pay serious money to support their habit. The first kind of game, with a hexagonal grid for a battlefield, assigns the player the role of company commander or strategist (though there are also tacticians), like the Squad Leader series, in which each counter (there are over a thousand of them) represents ten men, more or less. These games mostly take more than five hours to play, and some even go on for twenty or thirty hours. Their origins are in German *Kriegsspiel*, I think, those big nineteenth-century strategy boards that made it possible to play out wars before they began, or chess, which is an abstract war game. In the other kind of game, the player steps into the skin of a soldier, like in a play. The game consists of a day or a weekend spent in military exercises. There are lessons in handling all types of weapons, conferences of Vietnam veterans, mock battles, and even parachute jumps arranged by some organizations for their members. Whatever variant you choose, the simulations claim to be models of historical accuracy: the battles never happen in limbo but in concrete places, either in the past or in some predictable or fantasy future: Vietnam, Iran, Libya, Cuba, Colombia, El Salvador, Nicaragua, even Mexico are among the scenes of the skirmishes. Important to note: some battles take place in the United States itself, where the enemy is a hypothetical black or Chicano guerrilla force. The hexboard campaigns mostly feature World War II, though you can also find near-future wars, from the Sixth Fleet shooting up every living thing in the Mediterranean to a European-theater-only version of World War III, atomic bombs included. But most are of them are World War II games, with obvious Nazi iconography and perspectives. In their ads, for example, they promise the prospective player that if he plays well and is lucky, Operation Barbarossa will succeed, Rommel's tanks will reach Cairo, and the Ardennes Offensive will end in an honorable armistice. Both hobbies, the board games and the weekend games, have more than one dedicated journal and are supported by an infrastructure only conceivable in the United States. Incidentally, the publisher of the board games is now putting out computer war games. As far as I can tell, business is booming."

"But who plays?" asked Dr. Carvajal.

"That's the strangest thing. You'd think that only murderers and Ku Klux Klanners would show up for the live war games, but it turns out that it's popular among college graduates, housewives, yuppies, and people who are sick of jogging. Whereas the board games attract lazy fascists, military-history buffs, shy teenage boys, and even former chess players: I hear that Bobby Fischer has been playing Battle of Gettysburg for more than two years. Not against anyone, just by himself."

Dr. Carvajal nodded with a cold angelic smile.

"The world has taken a strange turn," he murmured. "Miniaturists always struck me as minions of the devil. All my life, I've believed that Evil practices her pirouettes on a small stage before making her debut. Frankly, compared to these gringo fetishes, our magazines seem like what they are: lame beasts."

"But they're alive," said José Arco. Then he asked me under his breath, "Where did you get all that?"

I said it was from the papers that Jan had been collecting.

"According to him, the John Birch Society is a sweet old folks' home compared to the gang at *Soldier of Fortune* magazine, who aren't just mercenaries by trade but the true creators of imperialist performance art, also known as happenings. The same can be said about all the businesses supporting board games. Avalon Hill, for example, publishes a magazine that you should take a look at someday: it's called *The General,* and it's the bible of armchair Mansteins, Guderians, and Kleists."

"Jan talked to me about Guderian once."

Dr. Carvajal was staring at us like a suicide rock.

"Jan is a friend of ours," I explained. "He says that . . . Guderian's tanks have to be stopped over and over—across a whole century, I guess, though I don't know whether that has to do with what we're talking about."

"Bloodbath lyricism," grumbled the doctor, and he waved his hand as if to say that none of it mattered a fig to him but that we could talk as long as we wanted.

José Arco, who liked to be contrary, kept his mouth shut after that. I spouted some nonsense about the first thing that came into my head, and our host told stories about highly respected doctor poets and government-official poets we'd never heard of. How sad, I thought in a flash of clarity or fear, someday I'll be telling stories about lumpen poets, and the people around me will wonder who those poor bastards were. Finally, when my friend's stubborn silence was beginning to get on my nerves, I asked to borrow a few magazines, ten at most, and Dr. Carvajal made no objection. "Do you plan to write an article for the paper?" I don't know why, but I lied: yes. "Then try to exaggerate only as much as you absolutely have to." The two of us smiled. José Arco began to pick out magazines.

Once we were outside, my friend said, "The poor bastard doesn't have a clue."

It was a clear night, and the moon in Dr. Carvajal's neighborhood looked like a sheet hung out to dry in the windy sky. The motorcycle had broken down, as usual, and we pushed it along, trading places every two blocks.

"Explain what you mean, please, because I have no clue either."

"I feel like killing somebody."

After a long time, he added, "I feel like getting a tattoo on my arm."

Now I was the one pushing the motorcycle.

"What kind of tattoo?"

"The hammer and sickle." His voice sounded dreamy and carefree. Good, I thought: it was just the night for dreams, and we had a long walk ahead of us. I laughed.

"No, man, how about this: I'LL LIVE IN MEMORY FOREVER. Don't you like that?"

"Fuck, it's weird, leaving that asshole's house I was super depressed but also super happy."

I said I didn't understand, and we were silent until it was his turn to take the motorcycle.

"Make that tattoo a Mexican flag with the hammer and sickle on it," he said.

I lit a cigarette. It was nice to walk without having to push the motorcycle. We were in a neighborhood of narrow streets, stunted trees, and three-story buildings.

"I'd like to get the fuck out of here once and for all," said José Arco. "With the motorcycle and my Mexican flag."

"Tell me what you didn't like about Dr. Carvajal."

"His skull face." He spoke each word with blind conviction. "He looked like a Posada skeleton taking the pulse of all the poor young poets."

"Yes," I said, "now that you mention it . . ."

"Fuck, he was the skeleton of Posada, dancing while he took the pulse of the whole country."

Suddenly I felt that there was an edge of truth to José Arco's words. I tried to piece together Dr. Carvajal's face, the living room of his apartment, the ordinary things in it, the way he greeted us and got up to look for the magazines, his eyes that might have been scrutinizing something else, somewhere else, as we were talking.

"I realized it when you were telling us all about the Yankee games. He didn't realize that I realized it."

"Realized what?"

"The way he was looking at us, looking at you, like everything you were saying was old news to him . . . For a second, I thought it was true, the old bastard knew everything . . ."

Without being aware of it, we had stopped walking. There was a change in the sky all of a sudden: somewhere in

Mexico City, it was raining, and to judge by the thunder and lightning, we would soon be getting drenched. My friend smiled. He was perched on the seat of the motorcycle, and he seemed to be waiting for the downpour.

"Just thinking about it scares me," I said.

"It's not such a big deal. Looks like it's going to rain."

"He did have a skull face, you're right," I said.

"Yeah, afterward I thought it wasn't that he knew everything but that nothing mattered to him."

"Maybe, maybe not."

"There are lots of guys like that. They call themselves 'sons of the Mexican Revolution.' They're interesting, but they're actually fucking sons of bitches, not sons of the revolution."

"Maybe, maybe not," I said as I looked up at the dark, dark, pitch-black sky. "We're going to get caught in the storm."

"I don't hate them. In fact, it's amazing to see how they deal with loneliness." José Arco held out his hands with the palms upraised. "In a very, very twisted way, they've gotten what they wanted: they're the absentee fathers of this country. A drop just fell on me." He raised the palm of his hand to his nose and sniffed it as if rain had more than one smell (it does).

"I don't know what to tell you. . . . This fucking piece-of-shit bike, we're going to get soaked . . ."

"I couldn't."

"You couldn't what?" The raindrops began to patter on

the dark body of a fifties Ford parked in front of us. We hadn't noticed it until now; it was the only car on the empty street.

"I could never be so alone, so silent, so disciplined about myself and my fate, pardon the expression."

"Fuck . . ."

A broad, bright smile appeared on José Arco's face.

"Come on, my friend's garage is around here. Let's see if he'll fix the bike and give us coffee."

Dear James Tiptree Jr.:

The rain teaches us things. It's night and it's raining:
the city spins like a shiny top, but some areas are opaque,
emptier; they're like flickering dots; the city spins happy
in the middle of the deluge, and the dots throb. From
where I am, they seem to swell like a feverish temple or
like black lungs with no notion of the shine that the rain
is trying to give them. Sometimes I have the impression
that the dots manage to touch: it's raining, there's
lightning, and an opaque circle brushes another opaque
circle, making a supreme effort. But that's as far as it
goes. Immediately they shrink into their own spaces and
keep throbbing. Maybe brushing each other is enough;
it's possible that the message, whatever it is, has been
sent. And so on, for hours or minutes, as long as the rain
lasts. This, I think, is a happy night. I read, I wrote, I
studied, I ate cookies and drank tea. Then I went out on
the roof to stretch my legs, and when it got dark and it

started to rain, I climbed up to the roof of the roof (in other words, the roof of my room) with an umbrella and binoculars, and I was there for almost three hours. It was then that I thought of you—I can't remember why now— and of the letter that I sent you quite a while ago. (I don't know whether you received it; to be safe, I'm sending this one to the Spiderman brothers' agency.) About that first letter . . . well, I just want to say that I sincerely hope you didn't take it the wrong way or you weren't offended that I addressed it to Alice Sheldon. I swear it wasn't a breach of trust. It's just that unlike many of your current readers, I already knew your earlier work, back when everybody said that James Tiptree Jr. was a retiree who had come late to writing. And I liked it. Later, of course, I was surprised when I found out that the name was actually a pseudonym—and according to some accounts more than a pseudonym, a heteronym—for the psychologist Alice Sheldon. A simple superimposition of images, you see. And Alice Sheldon happens to be a much prettier, warmer name. That's all. (Sometimes I imagine the retired Mr. Tiptree writing in a little house in Arizona. Why Arizona? I don't know. I must have read it somewhere. Maybe it was Fredric Brown, who lived in Arizona for a few years, more or less as a retiree, in all the exile and equilibrium that the word implies. For argument's sake, wouldn't it be better to maintain a correspondence with North American retirees than with science fiction writers? Could I convince them to send letters to the White House demanding an end to the policy of aggression toward Latin America? It's certainly possible, but let's not get ahead of ourselves.) The rain isn't stopping. While I was perched on the roof gazing through my binoculars at the dark rooftops of other buildings, a question came into my mind: how many science fiction novels have been written in Paraguay? On the surface, it seems like a stupid question, but it made so much sense to me just then that it kept coming back to me, like a catchy pop song. Were the closed windows of Mexico City really Paraguay? Were the storm and the rooftops that I was watching through the binoculars really the science fiction of Paraguay? (For half a mile all around, there were lights in very few windows, maybe something like ten or fifteen of them, and almost all on a strip of Insurgentes Sur; none of the lights were on rooftops.) At the time, the question struck me as terrifying. Now not so much. But now I'm sitting in my room, not outside in the rain. I don't know. I'll send you a postcard of Mexico City with this letter. It's a photograph, a shot taken from the Torre Latino-americana. You can see the whole city. It's daytime, around two in the afternoon, but the print or the photograph itself is slightly flawed: the image is fuzzy. It's what I felt tonight, in the dark. I'll keep you posted.

Yours,

Jan Schrella

The motorcycle-repair shop was a single room, six meters long by three wide. At the back, a door hanging half off its hinges led to an inner courtyard where garbage piled up. Margarito Pacheco, a.k.a. El Mofles, had been living there for two years, since the day he turned seventeen and left his mother's house, which actually was only about three blocks away, also in Peralvillo. He fixed motorcycles and sometimes cars, though he was a pretty bad car mechanic. He knew it, and he wasn't ashamed to admit it: the night that José Arco and I showed up at his shop pushing the Honda, it had been more than a year since he'd touched a car. His specialty was motorcycles, though there wasn't an abundance of work. Out of thrift or maybe because he liked it, he had set up house in the garage, though this was a detail that the unobservant visitor might miss: the only visible signs were a camp cot behind a heap of tires and a bookcase surrounded by old car calendars, oil calendars, and pinup calendars. The toilet was in the yard. He showered at his mother's house.

At first glance, he seemed like a shy kid, but he wasn't. He was missing all his upper teeth. Maybe that explains his initial reserve, his polite, monosyllabic responses to our questions, his enigmatic smiles when we laughed. This would go on until the stranger—in this case, me—said something that he found really interesting or funny. Then he would laugh openly or start to talk very fast, in a Spanish full of slang and words he invented as he went along. His eyes were big—too big—and as you got to know him, his sickly thin-ness became a strange beauty, gentle and asymmetrical. He had lost his teeth in a fight at fifteen. The mechanic's trade was something he had learned in that very garage, first watching and then helping a mechanic from Tijuana who, as El Mofles described him, might easily have been Castaneda's Don Juan. When the mechanic died, which was about two years ago, his wife didn't want anything to do with the shop, and in less than a week she'd gone back to where she was from. El Mofles had the keys to the shop, and he waited there for someone to come and claim it, or at least to charge rent. At first he slept on the floor; then he brought in the camp cot and his clothes. After a month, the only person who came by, other than a few clients, was a guy trying to sell him a stolen motorcycle. That was how he got started in the business.

When I met him, he had just two motorcycles in the shop, his own and the Aztec Princess, which was the Benelli that José Arco had told me about. I said I liked it. El Mofles said it was a good bike and it was odd that it was still here in the shop. Days later I realized what he'd meant, and it seemed like a sign blinking half hidden among the oil stains and the dirty floorboards of the shop, a sign I could heed or not. In the business of stolen motorcycles, El Mofles worked with two people, one who brought the bikes and one who took them. Always the same two people. And always at set times. At the beginning of the month, a bike would appear, and halfway through the month the guy with the money would come and the bike would leave the shop. With the Aztec Princess, the routine had been interrupted for the first time in two years. The buyer didn't turn up in fifteen days, or even a month, and the motorcycle was in danger of being orphaned or turned into spare parts and junk.

I bought it that very night.

You could say that the deal worked itself out. I didn't have money, but El Mofles didn't have a buyer either. I promised to pay him part when I got paid and the rest in two monthly installments. His counteroffer was better: I would give him whatever I could afford whenever I could afford it, and he would sell me the motorcycle for the price he had paid for it, on the condition that I take it that very night. As José Arco looked on, smiling, I accepted. I didn't have a driver's license—hell, I didn't even know how to drive—but I had blind faith in my luck and in the signs I thought I had glimpsed. If you had a phone, everything would be perfect, I said.

"A phone? Yeah, right, it's a miracle that we have electricity here."

I didn't ask whether he was referring to the neighbor-hood or the place. José Arco boiled water and made three Nescafés. From a plastic bag hanging on the wall, El Mofles took some cold quesadillas. He warmed them on a hot plate. They were stiff, of course, but they looked good. As he was heating them up, he told me that I should come in one of these days to give the motorcycle a coat of paint.

"I like it the way it is," I said.

"It's always a good idea with a stolen motorcycle. That's the way it's done."

"These quesadillas are great," said José Arco. "Did your mom make them?"

El Mofles nodded. Then he shook his head, and as if he could hardly believe it, he said, "I don't know why the fuck I didn't think to get rid of the inscription. I just realized."

"What inscription?"

"On the Aztec Princess. It's practically screaming that it's stolen."

"It's a nice inscription. The letters are even metallic."

"I have no idea why I didn't scrape it off."

"I like it this way," I said. "I'm not going to get rid of it."

The rain wasn't letting up outside. Sometimes gusts of wind shook the whole shop, as if it was about to be ripped from its foundations, and the doors groaned with a rasping sound that was like a laugh and then a sudden deep scream. It sounds like someone being beaten to death, muttered José Arco. We were serious all of a sudden, lost in the storm and our own thoughts, as if the space in between—that is, the shop and the words we could have been speaking—didn't exist. In the yard, the wind whipped the empty cans and papers.

After each sound, El Mofles looked up at the ceiling. Sometimes he paced back and forth with the cup of Nescafé in his hand, trying or pretending to read the grime-covered signs posted on the walls. Still, he didn't seem nervous. On the contrary. Though you could say it was a deceptive calm, no more than a surface calm: a remoteness neither arctic nor ignorant but like that of a Christian just released from his torments. The remoteness of a body that's been terribly beaten or utterly satiated.

"The world is beautiful, isn't it?" said El Mofles.

It was five in the morning when we left. My two friends spent a while teaching me the basic principles of motorcycle riding. According to them, the trick was not to be afraid of cars and to know how to accelerate, brake, and use the clutch. What about changing speeds? That's important, too. Try to keep your balance. Try to glance at stoplights every once in a while. Don't worry about the rain.

I went out into the yard to check the weather. The rain wasn't as intense anymore. I asked José Arco what would happen if we were outside when it started coming down hard again. He didn't answer. After El Mofles had tuned up the Honda, he asked us if we wanted to hear some poems he'd written. (Making these requests, El Mofles was like a village priest in the presence of the pope: he welcomed all criticism and never defended anything he'd written.) Of the five or six he read that night, there was one that I liked a lot: it was about his girlfriend, Lupita, and his mother watching from the distance as a building went up. The rest were pop-style poems: song lyrics, ballads. José Arco loved them. I didn't. When we leave, José Arco said, I'm going to tell you the best story El Mofles ever came up with.

"What is it?"

"It's the story of how Georges Perec, as a boy, prevented a duel to the death between Isidore Isou and Altagor in an old neighborhood of Paris."

"I'd rather read it."

"It isn't written, it's an oral story."

El Mofles smiled, blushing, wiped his hands on a rag, and put on water for the last round of Nescafé. Suddenly I realized that I was scared, panicked; I thought of a thousand different ways that things could end badly, seeing myself first at the police station and then at the hospital, every bone in my body broken. We drank our coffee. In silence I listened to the final instructions. When we went outside, the street looked dark and deserted. Without a word, José Arco got on my motorcycle and started it. The roar of the tailpipe made me shudder. Then he got on his bike, and we rolled down the street to the end of the block, testing the engines. We turned, with me always close behind, and returned to where El Mofles was waiting for us.

"You've made it like new," said José Arco. I was silent, all my senses focused on keeping the engine from stalling. Take care and come back soon, said El Mofles. Of course, said

José Arco. How do you feel, Remo? Scared shitless, I said. It was strange—the sound of our voices was muted, even the sound of the bikes seemed to come from far away; meanwhile the sounds of the sleeping street were magnified in my ears: cats, the first morning birds, water running in the pipes, some distant door, the snores of a man in a house down the block.

"All right, you'll get over it; we'll go slow, stay right next to each other."

"Okay," I said.

"See you around, Mofles."

"Good-bye."

We coasted out of the neighborhood as if we were on bicycles. Every so often, José Arco asked me how I was doing. Soon we left the empty streets of El Mofles's neighborhood and turned onto a wide avenue.

"Stick close to me," said José Arco.

The two motorcycles lurched forward. I felt as if somebody had given me a kick somewhere in my insides. My hands were sweating, and I was afraid they would slip off the handlebars. Several times I thought about braking, but I was prevented by the certainty that if I did, the Aztec Princess would be left lying abandoned in the street while I went home on the Metro. At first all I could see was the asphalt lane, interminable and full of silences suddenly broken, and the hazy outline of my friend and his Honda, sometimes moving ahead of me and other times letting me move ahead. Then, as if a curtain was drawn back in the middle of the desert, a hulking mass appeared on the horizon, gigantic but far in the distance, seeming to flicker or cycle through every shade of gray in the world through the fine mist of rain. What the hell is that? I screamed in my head. The Turtle of Death? The Great Beetle? The thing was as big as a hill, I calculated, and it was coming straight at us, propelled by pseudopods or perhaps on a cushion of steam. Its progress, from where I sat, was unrelenting. I didn't need to ask José Arco which way we were going.

"La Villa!" he called, pointing his finger at Godzilla.

"La Villa, La Villa!" I shouted happily.

Only then did I notice the cars passing us; the half-hidden stoplights, corroded by smog, flashing on and off at the corners; the shadowy figures moving along the sidewalk, even smoking cigarettes; the buses, lit up like riverboats, carrying workers to their jobs. In the middle of the street, a kid, drunk or high, called out to death and then fell to his knees, impassively watching the cars go by. From inside a coffee shop that had just opened its doors came the strains of a *ranchera*.

We stopped near the plaza in front of the basilica to stretch our legs and to see how I was doing so far on my first motorcycle ride. I told José Arco that a minute ago I'd been convinced that the basilica was a monster. Or a petrified atomic blast striding toward us. If that's what it was, wouldn't it be heading toward the center of the city? Maybe, I said, but still, we were in the way. Good thing you're all right. How is the Aztec Princess behaving? Isn't she a nice bike?

I don't know why, but the air seemed to be coming at us from a hole in the clouds. I lit a cigarette and said yes.

"Well, it wasn't an atomic bomb," said José Arco as he cast an eye over my motorcycle. "It was the castle of the Virgin of Guadalupe, mother of all, the great babe."

"Yes," I said watching the sunrise, which was only the faintest glow so far. "She's the one who saved me from getting into an accident."

"No, man, that was me and Mofles, we're pedagogues of the wheel."

I felt in my pockets for coins.

"Wait for me a minute, I'm going to make a phone call."

"All right."

Nearby I found a public phone and called Laura. After a long time, her mother picked up. I apologized for calling so early and asked if she would be so kind as to get Laura. It's urgent, I think; I don't know, I said, playing dumb. I wasn't tired, but I would have been happy to flop down on my mattress. The streets were bright, and next to me a couple of taxi drivers were talking about soccer—one liked Club América and the other preferred Guadalajara. When Laura came on the line, I apologized again, exactly as if I was back on the line with her mother, and then I told her that I loved her.

"It's hard to explain. I'm in love with you."

Laura said, "It's nice that you called."

"That's all I wanted to tell you, that I love you."

"Great," said Laura. "That's great."

We hung up, and I went back over to the motorcycles.

"Everything okay? Ready to go?"

"Yes," I said, "let's go."

"Do you think you can make it home?"

"Yeah, sure."

"I'll come with you anyway."

"There's no need. You must be tired."

"Tired? Me? No, man, and anyway, I still haven't told you the story of Isidore Isou and Altagor."

"What shit is that?"

"El Mofles's story, man, wake up."

We headed toward the center of the city, taking our time. The air finally cleared my head. It was nice to ride along on the bike and watch the streets and windows begin to wake up. People who'd been out all night drove their cars home or wherever, and workers drove their cars to work or piled into the vans or waited for the buses that would take them to work. The geometric landscape of the neighborhoods, even the colors, had a provisional look, filigreed and full of energy, and if you sharpened your gaze and a certain latent madness, you could feel sadness in the form of flying sparks, Speedy Gonzales slipping along the great arteries of Mexico City for no reason at all or for some secret reason. Not a melancholy sadness but a devastating, paradoxical sadness that cried out for life, radiant life, wherever it might be.

"It's a strange story," shouted José Arco. "I won't insult you by asking if you know who Isou and Altagor are."

"Go ahead and insult me, I have no idea."

"Really? Fucking Latin America and its fucking young intellectuals!" José Arco laughed.

"Well, Isou is French," I yelled. "And he writes visual poetry, I think."

"Cold, cold."

Then he said something that I didn't understand—it was in Romanian—and we passed a truck loaded with chickens and then another truck loaded with chickens and another and another. It was a convoy. The chickens poked their beaks through the mesh of their cages and shrieked like teenagers on the way to the slaughterhouse. Where is my mother hen? the chickens seemed to say. Where has my egg gone? My God, I thought, I don't want to crash. La Salud Poultry Farm. José Arco's Honda drew up an inch or so from mine.

"Isou is the Father of Lettrism and Altagor is the Father of Metapoetry!"

"Wonderful!"

"And they hate each other bitterly!"

We stopped at a red light.

"I don't know where the hell El Mofles reads these things. He didn't make it past the first year of high school."

Green.

"Where did you read them?" The Aztec Princess didn't move right away. It jolted forward.

"I go to the Librería Francesa! While the jackasses are lining up for Octavio Paz's lectures, I spend hours digging around in there! I'm basically a nineteenth-century gentleman!"

"And you never run into Mofles?"

"Never!"

A Mustang going sixty miles an hour drowned out José Arco's last words. Eventually I would learn that El Mofles only visited the Librería El Sótano, and then only occasionally. The story of Isou and Altagor and Georges Perec was very simple. Just after World War II, in a Paris still under rationing, Isou and Altagor met at one of the legendary cafés. Isou sat on the terrace to the far right and Altagor to the left, let's say. Still, each was aware of the other's presence. The tables in the middle were occupied by American tourists, famous painters, Sartre, Camus, Simone de Beauvoir, movie actors, and Johnny Hallyday.

"Johnny Hallyday, too?"

"That's El Mofles for you, the bastard."

And so our two phonetic poets sat in perfect anonymity. Only the two of them fully understood what was going on and knew themselves to be the Father of Metapoetry and the Father of Lettrism, greater enemies than the houses of Verona.

"According to El Mofles, they were both young and ambitious! *Vanitas vanitatum!*"

"Fucking Mofles!"

So after gloomily downing their pastis and munching their sandwiches, the only sustenance either of them would get that night, they called for the check, but one of them asked for it in metalanguage and the other in lettrist caló, and the next minute they refused to pay. Their aim, apart from getting themselves noticed by the tables in the middle, was to get the waiters to speak to them in the languages in which they'd been addressed. Sure enough, insults were soon flying. The waiters swore at them under their breath, trying not to call attention to themselves. Isou treated the waiters like ignorant slaves and mocked Altagor. The Father of Lettrism, on the other side of the terrace, loudly bewailed the narrow-mindedness of the waiters and shook his fist at Isou.

"What assholes!"

"Ha-ha-ha."

"Hee-hee-hee."

"They're Mofles's heroes!"

The appearance of Gaston, the maître d', a fierce warrior of the Maquis, put an end to the dispute. Gaston was a terror, and everybody knew it. Much to their chagrin, both poets paid up, and to make matters worse, they saw that they'd made fools of themselves in front of the select tables in the middle. Utterly crushed, Isou and Altagor left the café: it was then, out in the street, that they decided to meet in a duel to the death. (In their mutual despair, they believed that Paris wasn't big enough for both of them.) The time was set for that very morning on the Champs de Mars, near the Eiffel Tower. And that is where Georges Perec comes in.

"Do you know Georges Perec?"

"Yes, but I haven't read anything by him."

"He was one of the best," said José Arco very seriously; our motorcycles were going ten miles an hour along the very edge of the road.

"We look like two night-shift workers on our way home," I said.

"Basically," said José Arco.

According to El Mofles, Perec was a kid who rose with the sun. First thing in the morning, he snuck on tiptoe out of his grandparents' house, got on his bike, and hightailed it around the city, no matter the weather. The morning in question, he went pedaling around the Champs de Mars. And wouldn't you know it, the first person he runs into is Altagor, sitting on a bench and reciting one of his own poems for courage. Little Perec stops near him and listens. It goes like this: *Sunx itogmire ésinorsinx ibagtour onéor galire a ékateralosné.* Which to the boy's ears sounds the same as if ten years ago you and I and El Mofles had met Mary Poppins in person singing "Supercalifragilisticexpialidocious." According to El Mofles, little Perec—who despite his youth is painfully polite and pedantic—begins to applaud with barely contained enthusiasm, which attracts the attention of Altagor, who looks at him and asks *Veriaka e tomé?*

"Oh, my God, Mofles is too much."

Tumissé Arimx, answers the boy, and Altagor's resolve crumbles. He sees the boy as a portent, a sign telling him to keep working come hell or high water. So he gets up, dusts himself off, bows down to the boy as if before fate itself, and goes off to his room to sleep. Shortly after this, the boy runs into Isidore Isou, and the same kind of thing happens. Maybe Isou doesn't say a word to the boy. Maybe he just sees him riding his bike around the Champs de Mars and singing *Echoum mortine flas echoum mortine zam,* and that's all it takes. Years later, when Georges Perec wrote the account *I Remember,* for reasons unknown he forgot to include this story.

"Perec hasn't been translated into Spanish, and El Mofles doesn't speak French. I leave you with that mystery for breakfast."

All of Mexico City was bathed in a deep yellow light. We had arrived. I felt less like eating breakfast than like sleeping; with Laura, if possible. I pointed out to José Arco that I had seen worse in the last few days.

"El Mofles's universe is full of stories like that. I wonder if he might be responsible for one of those little magazines."

"We'll ask him," I said.

Then I left the motorcycle on the first-floor landing, maybe with the secret hope that it would be stolen, and I went up the stairs two at a time.

When I woke up, the first thing I saw was Jan's flushed face and Angélica Torrente's Greek profile smoking a Delicado and then Laura's serene, expectant smile, all connected by a kind of arc of energy, very fine and very black, an effect that I attributed to the sleep in my eyes, and finally, as I pulled the sheet up to my nose, I saw the open door and the plants in the corridor shuddering and the daughter of one of the tenants walking away with a roll of toilet paper in one hand and a transistor radio blaring in the other. Angélica Torrente had been here for an hour. The entire time, she'd been arguing with Jan. Of course, that wasn't why she'd come: the purpose of her visit was love and confessions. But things got off track, and the two of them found themselves arguing, sorrowfully and stubbornly, and though most of the time it was at the top of their lungs, they didn't manage to wake me. The problem was the table made of science fiction books. Jan had shown it to her with the beaming pride of a Chippendale collector, and Angélica, after studying it in astonishment and disgust, had decreed that it was nothing less than a slap in the face to literature in general and science fiction in particular. "Books should be on bookshelves, neatly organized, ready to be read or consulted. You can't treat them this way, like Meccano pieces or vulgar bricks!" Jan argued that many city dwellers under siege had relieved their hunger by masticating the pages of books: in Sevastopol in 1942, a young writer had ingested a good chunk of Proust's *In Search of Lost Time,* in the original French. Science fiction, Jan believed, was especially well suited to serendipitous bookcases, like the bookcase-table, for example, without being any less valued for the content of its pages or its tales of adventure. According to Angélica, this was idiotic and impractical in the extreme. Tables were for eating on, for spilling sauces on, for stabbing with knives in fits of rage. My God! was Jan's response, accompanied by a dismissive wave. That has nothing to do with anything! You don't get it! There are tablecloths!

After which there was an instant when they tried to move from words to deeds. For a fraction of a second, they met in an attempt at *lucha libre,* masks versus manes, that might have ended or climaxed with the two of them tangled on Jan's mattress, legs pressed to legs, arms wrapped around backs and shoulders, hands clawing, and jeans pulled down to knees. But it didn't happen. They just lunged at each other a few times, getting in a few jabs on the forearms, their breathing faster and the gleam in their eyes more intense. Then Laura arrived, and the argument lost steam and finally fizzled out.

Laura hardly noticed the table at all. "I saw a motorcycle on the landing," she said in a sibylline voice. "I bet it's Remo's."

"No, no, no," sighed Jan. "Absolutely not. My esteemed friend only knows how to ride a bicycle."

"How much do you want to bet?" Laura was like that; when she was sure about something, she would rather die than let her arm be twisted. Luckily for her, her convictions were few, though they were as sharp as a falcon's beak.

"But, my dear," said Jan, "up until yesterday he didn't have a motorcycle, so there's no way he could have one now."

"I'm sure it's his motorcycle."

"Unless"—Jan seemed doubtful—"he stole it, but even so, how can you steal a motorcycle when you don't know how to ride it?"

A vision of me buying the motorcycle and signing letters and contracts flashed through Jan's mind like a shout. It was a chilling prospect, as he would later confess to me, because he was forced to accept something that he'd never wanted to admit: our disastrous economic situation. If the motorcycle was mine, which was beginning to seem more and more likely, we would surely be up to our ears in debt for at least five years, and to make matters worse, I would need financial help, which meant that he would have to look for work.

"My God, I hope it isn't true," he said.

"It's a very nice motorcycle," said Laura.

"When I came up, I guess there was a motorcycle on the landing," said Angélica, "but it didn't look nice to me. It was an ugly old motorcycle."

"Why do you call it ugly?" asked Laura.

"Because I thought it was. An old motorcycle all covered in stickers."

"You must not have gotten a good look at it. It has character. And there aren't that many stickers on it. In fact, there's just an inscription, a really original one in metallic letters: 'Aztec Princess' . . . that must be its name."

"The name of the motorcycle."

"Such observant girls," said Jan.

"Listen, it's cheesy enough to give a motorcycle a name. But to call it Aztec Princess, ugghh," said Angélica.

"No, it can't be Remo's," said Jan. "But, Laura, you spent hours studying that motorcycle!"

Laura laughed and said yes, the hulking rusty thing out there on the landing had spoken to her: there was something about it that made her feel sad, like crying. Angélica said, "bullshit." Then I woke up.

Cautiously, I began to perform the delicate maneuver of getting dressed. The two girls had already seen Jan naked, and I guess they thought it would be bad manners to close their eyes or turn to face the wall while I was getting up. I didn't say anything. I put my pants on under the sheet and did the best I could.

"The motorcycle is mine."

"See?" said Laura.

"I bought it from a savage poet in Peralvillo. I'll pay for it when I have money."

"In other words, never," said Jan.

"I'll work more. I'll enter all the literary contests. I give myself a year to get famous and make the same money as somebody with a desk job at the bottom of the ladder. All this, of course, if I don't end up in jail first for riding without a license on a motorcycle that turned up out of nowhere."

"Stolen," said Jan.

"Exactly. What do you expect? But I didn't steal it! It fell into my hands by chance. Come on, can you imagine the Lone Ranger buying Silver at an auction? No, the Lone Ranger found Silver on the prairie. They found each other, and they hit it off. Same for Red Ryder. Only that ass Hop-along Cassidy would buy a new horse every year."

"But you don't know how to ride a motorcycle."

"I learned last night. It's not so hard. It's all in the head, really. License, police, stoplights, fear of cars—those are the hard parts. If you forget about all that, you can learn to ride a motorcycle in half an hour."

"Sure," said Angélica, "it's like the luck of the drunk. If you aren't afraid that something will happen to you, it won't."

"Most accidents are the fault of drunk drivers," whispered Jan.

"No, half-drunk, which is totally different. Half-drunk drivers are terrified of screwing up, so of course they do. If you're completely drunk, you're thinking of other things. Well, actually, total drunks hardly ever get into a car. They just fall into bed."

We kept talking for a while about my motorcycle and the dangers that could befall me riding it around a place like

Mexico City. Some of the advantages, according to everyone except for me, were speeding past motorcades and traffic jams and being on time to all my appointments and future jobs. But he isn't going to get a job, said Laura, with an enigmatic smile, he's going to write poems and win all the contests. That's right, I said, I won't need the motorcycle for that. Maybe when I've got writer's block, I'll go out and ride around. Contests? What contests? Jan asked hopefully. All of them, said Angélica. You'll ride to the post office on the motorcycle, and you'll sit on the manuscripts so they don't blow away. True, and it's only fitting, too, I said. One of the disadvantages was the price of gasoline, which none of us knew, even approximately.

And so on and so on, until Jan and Angélica left and I realized that something had to happen between Laura and me. Where are you going? I asked. I had always been in favor of Jan leaving the room, even if only once a day, but this time I would have preferred it if he'd stayed. The two of them looked happy. Jan had his arm around Angélica's waist, and she was petting his hair. The scene terrified me.

"To the landing," said Jan. "We're going to take a look at your motorcycle, and if we really feel like it, we'll head over to La Flor de Irapuato."

"Don't be long," I said.

When we were left alone, there was a silence as sudden and heavy as a concrete ball. Laura sat on Jan's mattress, and I stared out the window. Laura got up and came over to the window. I sat on my mattress. I stuttered something about the motorcycle and going to get a coffee at La Flor de Irapuato. Laura smiled and said nothing. There was no doubt in my mind: she was the most beautiful girl I had ever seen in my life. And the most direct.

"Last night you said you wanted to make love with me. That you were dying to do it. What's wrong?"

"I'm out of practice," I stuttered. "I want to do it, I want it more than anything, but I'm out of practice. Also, it's hard to explain, but I'm kind of wounded in action."

Laura laughed and asked me to tell her about it. Little by little, I started to feel better. I put on water for tea, I made a few banal remarks about the weather, and then I confessed that not long ago I'd been ruthlessly and repeatedly kicked in the testicles, a kind of Chilean memento, and that since then I'd been convinced that I would never get it up again, a predictable reaction from an admirer of the Goncourt brothers. Actually, I can get it up, I admitted, but only when I'm alone.

"Why did they kick you there?"

"Who knows? Jan and I were wandering around desperately looking for our friend Boris, and not only did we not find him, we got caught ourselves."

"What about Jan, did he . . . ?"

"That's right, we both got thrashed. He was yelling as loud as me."

"But Jan has normal erections," said Laura. "I know that for a fact."

Laura had never seemed so pretty and so terrible. For a

173

second, I felt a wave of jealousy and fear. At what point had the hypocritical little satyr stolen my girlfriend?

"Really?" I said, with an icy smile.

Laura told me then that the night of the party in our room Jan and Angélica had made love. I must have been very drunk or high or depressed or immersed in López Velarde, because I didn't notice. Angélica felt sick, and her sister and Jan took her to the bathroom. Really, it was very stuffy in our room. In one of the chicken coops where clothes were hung up to dry, Laura bumped into Lola Torrente, José Arco, and Pepe Colina. Angélica and Jan had vanished. César was pretty drunk, and he wanted to leave. He begged, pleaded, claimed he was about to vomit—poor César, but too bad for him. Laura absolutely refused. In a corner full of pails, buckets of water, and empty boxes of detergent, César tried to make love to her as she looked over the railing. He was out of luck. Laura kept wandering sleepily around the roof (like the princess, candle in hand, who roams the castle of the prince she is to marry!) until on one of her rounds she came to what Jan cheerfully called the latrines. There she hesitated, and soon she heard a muffled noise coming from one of them. She thought that Angélica might be sicker than she'd seemed and went to investigate. Nothing could be further from the truth. Jan was sitting on the toilet, his pants around his ankles, and in the fingers of his left hand he held a match. Kneeling over him, Angélica was mounted on his erect cock. Every so often, when the match burned the tips of his fingers, Jan dropped it and lit another one. Discreetly, Laura returned to the others. The next day, Angélica told her what she already knew, plus some additional details.

"Phew! That's a relief."

"What's a relief? That your best buddy is still in working order, despite the beating?"

"Don't be vulgar. I thought you had slept with Jan."

"No, I went back with César to the place with the soap. A cozy spot—you'll have to show it to me by daylight. There I forced him to *penetrate* me. We almost fell over the parapet. It was quick, really quick. César was drunk and depressed. I was thinking of you, I felt really good. It was like I couldn't stop laughing inside, I think."

"Why didn't you tell me? That morning we talked for hours . . ."

"It was none of your business. Also, I was tired and I was having a good time with you, so why start an argument?"

"I wouldn't have argued. I would have cried. Shit."

"Silly, it was a kind of good-bye. I think I had already decided that we were done. Poor César." She sighed wickedly. "I wasn't even saying good-bye to him, but to his penis. Ten inches. I measured it myself with my mother's measuring tape."

"Shitshitshit. I'll never let you come near me with a measuring tape."

"I won't, I swear."

Dear Philip José Farmer:

Wars can be ended with sex or religion. Everything seems to indicate that there are no other citizen alternatives; these are dark days, heaven knows. We can set aside religion for now. That leaves sex. Let's try to put it to good use. First question: what can you in particular and American science fiction writers in general do about it? I propose the immediate creation of a committee to centralize and coordinate all efforts. As a first step— call it preparing the terrain—the committee must select ten or twenty authors for inclusion in an anthology, choosing those who have written most radically and enthusiastically about carnal relations and the future. (The committee should be free to select who they like, but I would presume to suggest the indispensable inclusion of entries by Joanna Russ and Anne McCaffrey; maybe later I'll explain why, in another letter.) This anthology, to be titled something like *American Orgasms in Space* or *A Radiant Future,* should focus the reader's attention on pleasure and make frequent use of flashbacks—to our times, I mean—to chart the path of hard work and peace that it has been necessary to travel to reach this no-man's-land of love. In each story, there should be at least one sexual act (or, lacking that, one episode of ardent and devoted camaraderie) between Latin Americans and North Americans. For example: legendary space pilot Jack Higgins, commander of the *Fidel Castro,* participates in interesting physical and spiritual encounters with Gloria Díaz, a navigation engineer from Colombia. Or: shipwrecked on Asteroid BM101, Demetrio Aguilar and Jennifer Brown spend ten years practicing the Kama Sutra. Stories with a happy ending. Desperate socialist realism in the service of alluring, mind-blowing happiness. Every ship with a mixed crew and every ship with its requisite overdose of amatory activity! At the same time, the committee should establish contact with the rest of American science fiction writers, those who're left cold by sex or who won't touch it for reasons of style, ethics, market appeal, personal preference, plot, aesthetics, philosophy, etc. They must be taught to see the importance of writing about the orgies that future citizens of Latin America and the U.S. can take part in *if we take action now.* If they flatly refuse, they must be convinced, at the very least, to write to the White House to ask for a cease in hostilities. Or to pray along with the bishops of Washington. To pray for peace. But that's our backup plan, and we'll keep it in under wraps for now. In closing, let me tell you how much I admire your work. I don't read your novels; I devour them. I'm seventeen, and maybe someday I'll write decent science fiction stories. A week ago, I lost my virginity.

Warmly,
Jan Schrella,
alias Roberto Bolaño

MEXICAN MANIFESTO

aura and I didn't make love that afternoon. We tried, but it didn't happen. Or at least that's what I thought at the time. Now I'm not so sure. We probably did make love. That was what Laura said, and she was the one who introduced me to the world of public bathhouses, which, beginning that day and for a long time after, I would associate with pleasure and play.

The first was definitely the best. It was called the Gimnasio Moctezuma, and in the lobby some unknown artist had painted a mural of the Aztec emperor up to his neck in a pool. Around the edges of the pool, near the monarch but much smaller, smiling men and women washed. Everyone seemed cheerful, except for the king, who stared out of the mural as if pursuing the unlikely spectator with wide, dark eyes in which many times I thought I glimpsed terror. The water of the pool was green. The stones were gray. In the background, mountains and storm clouds were visible.

The attendant at the Gimnasio Moctezuma was an

orphan, and that was his main topic of conversation. On our third or fourth visit, we became friends. He couldn't have been more than eighteen; he wanted to buy a car, so he was saving everything he could, basically his tips, which were few and far between. According to Laura, he was half retarded. I liked him. At every public bathhouse, there's a fight at some point. At this place, we never saw or heard a single one. The clients, conditioned by some unknown mechanism, followed the attendant's instructions to the letter. And the truth is that few people came, which is something I'll never be able to explain, because it was a clean, relatively modern place, with private cubicles for steam baths, and bar service to the cubicles, and, most important, it was cheap.

It was there, in Cubicle 10, that I saw Laura naked for the first time, and all I managed to do was smile and touch her shoulder and say that I didn't know which tap to turn to make steam come out. The cubicles, though it would be more accurate to call them private rooms, were a set of two tiny compartments connected by a glass door; in the first, there was usually a divan or old sofa (shades of psychoanalysis and the brothel), a folding table, and a coatrack; the second room was the steam bath properly speaking, with a hot- and cold-water shower and a tile bench built into the wall, under which the steam pipes were hidden.

Moving from one room to the next was extraordinary, especially if it was so steamy in the inner room that we couldn't see each other. Then we would open the door and come into the divan room, where everything was sharp and clear, trailing clouds of vapor like the vanishing filaments of a dream. Lying there hand in hand, we listened or tried to listen to the barely perceptible sounds of the Gimnasio as our bodies cooled. Chilled nearly to the bone, deep in silence, at last we could hear the rumble that issued from floor and walls, the feline purr of hot-water pipes and boilers in some secret part of the building, fueling the enterprise.

"Someday I'll go exploring around here," said Laura.

She had more experience in trips to public bathhouses, which was easy enough, since I had never crossed the threshold of a place like this before. Nevertheless she claimed to know nothing about the baths. Or not enough. She had been with César a few times and, before César, with a guy twice her age, someone to whom she occasionally alluded mysteriously. In total she hadn't been more than ten times, all to the same place, the Gimnasio Moctezuma.

Together, on the Benelli, which I had mastered by now, we tried to make the rounds of every bathhouse in Mexico City, driven by an all-consuming urge that was a mixture of love and play. We never managed it. In fact, the more places we visited, the wider the abyss that yawned around us, the greater the black stage set of the public baths. Just as the hidden faces of other cities may be theaters, parks, docks, beaches, labyrinths, churches, brothels, bars, cheap movie houses, old buildings, and even supermarkets, the hidden face of Mexico City is its enormous network of public baths, legal, semilegal, and underground.

Our strategy as we set off on this quest was simple: I

asked the attendant at the Gimnasio Moctezuma to give me
the addresses of a few cheap bathhouses. He passed me five
business cards and wrote down the street names and numbers of a dozen different establishments. These were the
first. After each one, the search branched countless times.
Schedules varied as widely as facilities. Some spots we came
to at ten in the morning and left at lunchtime. These, as a
rule, were bright, crumbling places, where sometimes we
could hear the laughter of adolescents and the coughs of lost,
lonely men who, after a while, feeling better, began to sing
boleros. Here the motto seemed to be limbo, a dead child's
closed eyes. They weren't very clean places, or maybe the
cleaning was done after midday. At others we made our appearance at four or five in the afternoon and didn't leave
until nightfall. (This was our most common practice.) Bathhouses at this time of day seemed to luxuriate—or languish—
in a permanent dusk. An artificial dusk, I mean: a dome or a
palm tree, the closest thing to a marsupial pouch, welcome
at first but gradually coming to weigh on visitors like a tomb-
stone. The busiest time for bathhouses was seven, seven
thirty, eight at night. On the sidewalk by the door, young
men stood guard talking baseball and the latest hits. The
hallways echoed with the grim jokes of workers just out of
factories and shops. In the lobby, the old queers, birds of
passage, called each of the receptionists and the loafers whil-
ing away the time in chairs by their first names or noms de
guerre. Wandering the hallways, feeding one's indiscreet curiosity in small doses, or pinches, never failed to be highly

instructive. Like landslides or earthquake cracks, the open or half-open doors presented vivid tableaux to the lucky observer: groups of naked men where any movement or action was courtesy of the steam; adolescents lost like jaguars in a labyrinth of showers; the tiny but terrifying gestures of athletes, weightlifters, and lone men; a leper's clothes hanging on a hook; little old men drinking Lulú and smiling, propped against the wooden door to the sauna . . .

It was easy to make friends, and we made them. Couples, after meeting a few times in the hallway, felt obliged to greet each other. This was due to a kind of heterosexual solidarity; in many of the public bathhouses, women were an absolute minority, and it wasn't unusual to hear extravagant tales of assaults and harassment, though the truth is that those stories weren't always trustworthy. Friendships like this never went further than a beer or a drink at the bar. At the baths, we said hello, or at most we got neighboring rooms. After a while, the first couple to finish knocked at the other couple's door, and, without waiting for a reply, announced that they would be at Restaurant X. Then the second couple emerged, stopped by the restaurant, had a few drinks, and that was it until their next encounter. Sometimes the couple shared confidences, the woman or the man, especially if they were married but not to each other; they'd tell their life stories, and you'd have to nod, say that's love, that's life, that's fate, that's kids. Sweet but boring.

The other, more troublesome kind of friends were those who came right into your private room. They could be as boring as the first kind, but much more dangerous. They turned up with no warning, just knocked at the door— a strange, quick knock—and said let us in. They were hardly ever alone; usually there were three of them, two men and a woman, or three men; the reasons offered for their visit were usually implausible or stupid: they wanted to smoke a little weed, which they couldn't do in the collective showers, or they wanted to sell some random thing. Laura always let them in. The first few times, I got tense, ready to fight and fall bloodstained to the tiles. I thought it was only logical that they had come to rob us or rape Laura or even to rape me, and I was about to jump out of my skin. Somehow the visitors knew that, and they spoke to me only when they had to or when it would've been rude not to. All propositions, deals, and whisperings were addressed to Laura. It was she who opened the door, it was she who asked what the fuck they wanted, it was she who let them into the little divan room. (I listened from the steam room as they sat down, first one, then the other, then the other; Laura's back, very still, was visible through the glass door that separated the steam room from the anteroom, which had suddenly become a place of mystery.) Finally I got up, wrapped a towel around my waist, and went in. A man and two boys or a man and a boy and a girl nodded uncertainly when they saw me, as if from the very beginning and against all logic they had come here for Laura and not for both of us; as if they had expected to find only her. They sat on the divan, their dark eyes not missing a single one of her movements, while their hands

186

rolled joints as if of their own accord. The conversations seemed coded in a language I didn't know, certainly not the slang I spoke with my friends, though now I can hardly remember it, but a much more affectionate kind of talk in which each word and each sentence had a trace of burials and holes. (Once when Laura was there, Jan said that it might be Air Hole, one of the bizarre manifestations of the Immaculate Grave. Maybe, maybe not.) In any case, I talked, too, or I tried. It wasn't easy, but I tried. Sometimes, along with the weed, they brought out bottles of alcohol. The bottles weren't free, but we didn't pay for them. Our visitors were in the business of selling marijuana, whiskey, and turtle eggs in the private rooms, rarely with the blessing of the attendant or the cleaning people, who chased them relentlessly; that was why it was so important for them to be let in by somebody; they also sold performances, which was how they really made their money, or arranged for private shows in their clients' bachelor apartments. The repertoire of these traveling companies could be meager or extremely varied, but the basic elements of the staging were always the same: the older man remained on the divan (thinking, I suppose), while the boy and the girl, or the two boys, followed the spectators into the steam room. As a rule, the performance lasted no more than half an hour or three-quarters of an hour, with or without the participation of the spectators. When the time was up, the man on the divan opened the door and, coughing in the steam that immediately tried to creep in from the other room, informed the respected audience that the show was over. Encores were expensive, even if they lasted only ten minutes. The boys showered quickly, and then the man handed them their clothes, which they put on over skin that was still wet. In the last few minutes, the hangdog but enterprising artistic director made sure to offer the satisfied spectators delicacies from his basket or bag: whiskey served in little paper cups, joints rolled with an expert hand, and turtle eggs that he opened with the enormous nail festooning his thumb and which, once in the cup, he sprinkled with lemon and chile powder.

In our room, things were different. They talked in soft voices. They smoked marijuana. They let time go by, checking their watches every so often, until their faces were covered with droplets of sweat. Sometimes they touched each other, everybody touched each other, which was inevitable anyway if we were all sitting on the divan, and the brushing of legs, of arms, could become painful. It wasn't the pain of sex but of something irretrievably lost or a single small hope wandering, walking, the country of Impossible. If they were people we knew, Laura invited them to undress and come with us into the steam room. They hardly ever accepted. They just wanted to smoke and drink and listen to stories. To rest. After a while, they closed their bag and left. Then, two or three times in the same evening, they came back, and the routine was always the same. If Laura was in the mood, she let them in; if not, she didn't even bother to tell them through the door to fuck off. Relations were at all times harmonious, except for one or two isolated incidents. I sometimes think they were fond of Laura long before they got to know her.

One night the old man who brought them (this time there were three of them, an old man and two boys) offered us a show. We had never seen one. How much does it cost? I asked. Nothing. Laura said they could come in. The steam room was cold. Laura took off her towel and turned the tap on: the steam began to issue from floor level. I had the feeling that we were in a Nazi bathhouse and we were about to be gassed; this feeling got stronger when the two boys came in, very thin and dark-skinned, and, bringing up the rear, the old pimp in nothing but an indescribably dirty pair of undershorts. Laura laughed. The boys looked at her, a little inhibited, standing in the middle of the room. Then they laughed, too. Between Laura and me, and without taking off his horrible underthings, the old man sat down. Do you want to just watch, or do you want to take part? Watch, I said.

"We'll see," said Laura, who liked puns.

Then, as if following a command, the boys knelt and began to soap each other's sex. Their movements, practiced and mechanical, betrayed weariness and a series of quiet tremors that it was easy to connect to Laura's presence. A minute went by. The room grew thick with steam again. The actors, still engaged in their initial activity, nevertheless seemed frozen: kneeling face-to-face but in a grotesquely artistic way, masturbating each other with their left hands and keeping their balance with their right. They looked like birds. Tin birds. They must be tired, they can't get it up, said the old man. It was true, the soaped cocks only pointed timidly up-ward. Is that the best you can do, boys? asked the old man. Laura laughed again. How are we supposed to concentrate if you keep laughing? said one of the boys. Laura got up, went around them, and leaned on the wall. Now the tired per-formers were between us. I felt that time, inside of me, was splitting open. The old man whispered something. I looked at him. His eyes were closed, and he seemed to be asleep. We haven't slept for so long, said one of the boys, letting go of his companion's penis. Laura smiled at him. Next to me, the old man began to snore. The boys smiled in relief and re-laxed into more comfortable positions. I heard their bones creak. Laura slid down the wall until her buttocks touched the tiles. You're very thin, she said to one of them. Me? So is he and so are you, replied the boy. The whistle of the steam made it hard to hear their voices sometimes, they were so low. Laura's body, her back against the wall, her knees bent, was covered in sweat: drops rolled down her nose, her neck, ran between her breasts, and even hung from the hairs of her pubis, where they fell onto the hot tiles. We're melting, I murmured, and immediately I felt sad. Laura nodded. How sweet she looked. Where are we? I wondered. With the back of my hand, I wiped away the droplets that were falling from my eyebrows into my eyes and blinding me. One of the boys sighed. I'm so tired, he said. Sleep, said Laura. It was strange: it seemed as if the lights were fading, growing dim; I was afraid I would pass out; then I guessed that it must be all the steam that was making the colors shade into something darker. (As if we were watching the sunset with no windows, I thought.) Whiskey and pot don't mix.

"Don't worry, Remo my love, everything is fine," Laura said, as if reading my thoughts.

And she smiled again, not a mocking smile, not as if she were amused, but a terminal smile, a smile caught between a sense of beauty and pain, though not ordinary beauty and pain but beauty and pain on a tiny scale, paradoxical dwarfs, roving and elusive dwarfs.

"Relax, my beloved, it's just the steam."

The boys, ready to believe that anything Laura said was irrefutable, nodded repeatedly. Then one of them dropped to the tiles, his head on his arm, and fell asleep. I got up, careful not to wake the old man, and I went over to Laura; crouching beside her, I buried my face in her damp, fragrant hair. I felt Laura's fingers stroking my shoulder. Soon I realized that Laura was playing—very gently, but it was a game: her little finger brushed my shoulder, then her ring finger, and they greeted each other with a kiss; then the thumb appeared, and the two of them, little finger and ring finger, fled down my arm; the thumb was left alone, master of the shoulder, and it fell asleep, even eating some vegetable that grew there, I think, because the thumbnail dug into my flesh, until the little finger and the ring finger returned, accompanied by the middle finger and the index finger, and together they scared away the thumb, which hid behind an ear, spying from above on the bullying fingers, without realizing why it had been kicked out, while the others danced on my shoulder, and drank, and made love, and lost their balance they were so drunk, plummeting down my back, an accident that allowed Laura to hug me and graze my lips with her lips, while the four fingers, bruised and battered, climbed back up, clinging to my vertebrae, and the thumb watched without ever considering leaving his ear, which he'd grown fond of by now. Head to head, we laughed without making a sound. You're shining, I whispered. Your face is shining. Your eyes. The tips of your nipples. You, too, said Laura. You're a little pale, maybe, but you're shining. It's the steam mixed with sweat. The boy watched us in silence. Do you really love him? he asked. His eyes were big and black. I sat down on the floor, close against Laura. Yes, she said. He must love you like crazy, said the boy. Laura laughed. Yes, I said. He'd have to, said the boy. You're right, I'd have to, I said. Do you know the taste of steam mixed with sweat? It depends on each person's particular taste, doesn't it? The boy lay down next to his companion, on his side, his temple resting directly on the tiles, not closing his eyes. His cock was hard now. His knees touched Laura's legs. He blinked a few times before he spoke. Let's fuck a little, he said. If you want to. Laura didn't answer. The boy seemed to be talking to himself. Do you know what steam mixed with sweat tastes like? What it really tastes like? What does it taste like? The heat was putting us to sleep. The old man had slid down until he was lying on the bench. The sleeping boy had curled into a ball, and one of his arms was around the waist of the one who was talking to us. Laura got up and looked down at us for a long time. I thought that she would turn on the shower, with tragic results for those who were sleeping so peacefully. It's hot, she said. It's unbearably hot. If you weren't here (she meant the trio), I would order a soda from the bar. You can, I said. They won't come in here, they'll hand it to you at the door. No, said Laura, it isn't that. The truth is, I don't know what I want. Should I turn off the steam? No. The boy, his head turned to the side, stared at my feet. Maybe I want to make love with you, said Laura. Before I could respond, the boy uttered a laconic no, almost without moving his lips. I was joking, said Laura. Then she knelt down beside him, and with one hand she stroked his buttocks. I watched—it was a fleeting and disturbing sight—as drops of the boy's sweat were transferred to Laura's body and vice versa. The long fingers of her hand and the boy's buttocks glistened identically. You must be tired. The old man is crazy. What was he thinking, asking you to fuck here?

So that we could watch, I reminded her. Laura didn't hear me. Her hand slid over the boy's buttocks. It isn't his fault, the boy whispered. He's forgotten what it's like to sleep in a bed. And what it's like to put on clean underwear, added Laura with a smile. He'd be better off wearing nothing, like Remo. Yes, I said, it's more comfortable. Less cramped, said the boy, but it's wonderful to put on clean white briefs. Tight ones, but not the kind that pinch. Laura and I laughed. The boy scolded us gently: Don't laugh, I'm serious. His eyes looked blurred, gray eyes like cement in the rain. Laura grabbed his cock with both hands and tugged. I heard myself saying should I turn off the steam? but my voice was faint and distant. Where the fuck does your manager sleep? asked Laura. The boy shrugged. You're hurting me a little, he whispered. I took Laura by an ankle; with the other hand, I wiped away the sweat that was getting in my eyes. The boy rose to a sitting position, moving carefully, trying not to wake his companion, and kissed Laura. I bent my head to see them better: the boy's thick lips sucked at Laura's closed lips, on which there was barely the hint of a smile. I half closed my eyes. I had never seen her smile so peacefully. Suddenly the steam hid her. I felt a kind of distant terror: fear that the steam would kill Laura? When their lips parted, the boy said that he didn't know where the old man slept. He raised a hand to his neck and made a slicing motion. Then he stroked Laura's neck and drew her even closer. Laura's body, elastic, adapted to the new posture. Her gaze was fixed on the wall, what she could see of the wall through the steam, her torso thrust forward, her breasts brushing the boy's chest or pressing gently against it, the steam hiding or partially obscuring them, turning them silver or submerging them in something like a dream. Finally I couldn't see her at all. First a shadow on a shadow. Then nothing. The room seemed about to explode. I waited for a few seconds, but nothing changed; in fact, I had the impression that the steam was getting even thicker. (I wondered how the fuck the old man and the other boy could keep sleeping.) I reached out a hand; I touched Laura's back, arched over what I guessed must be the boy's body. I got up and took two steps along the wall. I heard

Laura calling me. Remo, Remo . . . What do you want? I asked. I'm drowning. I retraced my steps, less careful than I had been moving forward, and I bent down, feeling around in the spot where I guessed she must be. All I felt were the hot tiles. I thought that I was dreaming or going crazy. Laura? Next to me, I heard the boy's voice: anybody can tell you that steam tastes different when it's mixed with sweat. I got up again, this time ready to kick out blindly as long as I hit someone, but I restrained myself. Turn off the steam, said Laura from somewhere. I stumbled to the bench as best I could. When I bent down to find the taps, I heard the old man snoring almost in my ear. He's still alive, I thought, and I turned off the steam. At first nothing happened. Then, before silhouettes were visible again, someone opened the door and left the steam room. I waited. Whoever it was in the other room was making quite a bit of noise. Laura, I called softly. No one answered. At last I could see the old man, who was still asleep. On the floor were the two performers, one in the fetal position and the other stretched out. The boy who couldn't sleep before seemed really to be asleep. I jumped over them. In the divan room, Laura was already dressed. She threw me my clothes without saying a word. What's the matter? I asked. Let's go, said Laura.

We met the same trio a few more times, once in the same bathhouse and another time at a bathhouse in Azcapotzalco, the bathhouse from hell, as Laura called it, but things were never the same. At most we smoked a cigarette and *adiós*.

For a long time, we kept coming back to these places. We

could have made love elsewhere, but there was something about the bathhouse route that attracted us like a magnet. Crazy things were always happening, of course—men running amok down hallways, a rape attempt, a raid—all of which we were lucky or cunning enough to navigate. The cunning was Laura's; the luck was the solidarity of bathers. Out of all the bathhouses together, now a jumble that I confuse with Laura's smiling face, we extracted the certainty of our love. Best of all, maybe because we did it there for the first time, was the Gimnasio Moctezuma, to which we always returned. The worst was a place in Casas Alemán, fittingly called the Wandering Dutchman, which was the closest thing possible to a morgue. A triple morgue: of hygiene, of the proletariat, and of bodies. Though not of desire.

I still have two indelible memories of those days. The first is a series of images of Laura naked (sitting on the bench, in my arms, under the shower, lying on the divan, thinking) until she disappears completely in a growing cloud of steam. The End. Fade to white. The second is the mural at Gimnasio Moctezuma. Moctezuma's unreadable eyes. Moctezuma's neck suspended over the surface of the pool. The courtiers (or maybe they weren't courtiers) laughing and talking, trying with all their might to ignore whatever it is the emperor sees. The flocks of birds and clouds mingling in the background. The color of the stones around the pool, surely the saddest color I saw in the course of our expeditions, comparable only to the color of some gazes, workers in the hallways, whom I no longer remember, but who were surely there.